EDGE OF THE DESERT

EDGE OF THE DESERT

L. P. Holmes

GUNSMOKE

First published in the US by Lancer Books

This hardback edition 2013
by AudioGO Ltd
by arrangement with
Golden West Literary Agency

ISBN 978 1 471 32164 1

British Library Cataloguing in Publication Data available.

Printed and bound in Great Britain by
TJ International Limited

Chapter ONE

THROUGH THE PULLMAN window at her elbow, the black-haired girl in the third coach of the *Overland Limited* watched a tide of sunset shadow spill down across a distant range of darkening mountains to shroud the on-running sweep of the sagebrush desert with a chill dusk. Having looked at a great deal of open country through such windows during the better part of the past week, she had now had enough of it and was restlessly anxious to be done with train travel for a while. However, she mused thankfully, from what the conductor had told her not long before, the desired break was close at hand. Her immediate destination, the town of Battle Mountain, was but minutes ahead.

Battle Mountain! Hardly a name to suggest peace and quiet. Playing with this fancy, she frowned wryly, stung with an uneasy moment of wonder that she, Miss Sherry Gault, fresh from the sedate East, should be speeding toward such a place on the humming wheels of the *Limited*.

Pressed though she was with impatience and a growing weariness, she sat quietly, a slender figure, her shoulders swaying to the swing of the speeding coach with an easy, natural grace. In spite of the wear and tear of some three thousand miles of steady journeying, plus day and night limitations of meager quarters and conveniences, she still managed to look crisp and well groomed.

She had her gear packed, ready to leave the train on notice, though she had allowed herself one comfort—she remained bare-headed, her hat on the seat beside her. And the coach lights, coming on now against the swift-gathering gloom, reflected rich glints in the thick folds of her hair.

Her features, just missing delicacy in line, were composed with a cool self-reliance, and out of deeply blue, faultlessly clear eyes, her glance was direct and prideful. Her mouth was softly curved and expressive, balanced by a chin that carried a tilt of independence and spirit. Here, in anybody's fair judgment, sat a young lady possessed of good looks, good taste, and a mind of her own.

Beyond the coach window, full blackness had come quickly down, smudging out all detail until it seemed the train was rushing through an inky void that had no limit or end. But when a light came presently forward out of the dark distance, followed by a growing cluster of them, perspective returned to the night world.

Flowing back from the engine came the wailing cry of its whistle. Compressed air hissed, and brakes took hold. The train's onward hurry lessened. Couplings creaked and groaned, and the clacking tempo of wheels over rail joints became a slowing beat.

6

Along the length of the coach a brakeman called "Battle Mountain! Next stop Battle Mountain!"

A porter appeared. "Your station, Missy?"

Sherry smiled up at him. "Yes. My station."

She donned her hat and rose to her feet, her gray wool traveling coat across her arm.

"Best you put that on, Missy," warned the porter. "Nights mighty cold hereabouts."

She let him help her don the coat, then went along the aisle, the porter following with her two grip sacks. The brakeman had lifted the platform and opened the outer door of the vestibule, and here was a rush of chill air to make her catch her breath and shrink deeper into the folds of her coat as the train eased to a panting halt. The porter's aiding hand guided her off the coach steps. He put her grip sacks beside her and glanced around worriedly.

"Ain't nobody set to meet you, Missy? This kind of town, there oughta be somebody."

His concern was genuine and won him the dollar she had ready for him.

"I'll be all right," she said confidently. "Thank you for your kindness."

Up front the engine bell swung impatiently. The whistle shrilled two short notes. Engine exhaust blasted the night sky, and the train began to move. The porter stepped aboard.

Gathering speed, the *Limited* bored away into the further west, the long flare of its headlight

7

fleeing before it, its whistle a dying echo in the distance. And now, much of the assurance Miss Sherry Gault had shown the porter frittered suddenly away. For this desert night was very lonely, very big, and very cold.

Footsteps crunched on cinders, and a man's tall figure loomed beside her. His words fell in a quiet drawl. "I'm hoping you are Miss Sherry Gault?"

Startled, she was touched with a small moment of panic, which eased somewhat when she realized that here was someone who knew her name, surprising as that was.

"Why . . . yes," she admitted carefully. "I am Sherry Gault. You are . . . Francis Quinnault?"

"No—thank God!" The words carried a bite of strong feeling. "No, I'm not Quinnault. I'm Luke Casement, foreman and riding boss of the Clear Creek Ranch. I've been meeting every westbound Limited for the past week, waiting for you to arrive. Friend Quinnault hung around for a couple of days, then gave up. Maybe because it was keeping him too long away from his favorite whiskey bottle. Being as I stuck it out, I figure I've the right to talk with you."

Sherry stiffened. "A talk? For what reason? I don't know you. I never heard of you before."

"True enough. But now you have. Here I am, right in front of you, and now you know my name too. The talk will be for your own good, as well as

8

that of a lot of other people. We can have it over the supper table at the Humboldt House, where you'll be staying the night, as it's the best place in town. Let's get along over there."

A shred of that initial panic returned. This fellow—this Luke Casement—was moving entirely too fast for Sherry's peace of mind. Her protest deepened, and she voiced it coldly.

"You needn't concern yourself. I can manage my own affairs—and prefer to."

"No," he said bluntly. "No, you can't manage. Not if the word going around is true. Not if you're really considering selling one of the best ranches in the state on Francis Quinnault's advice. For Jack McCord's memory deserves something better than that."

He seemed to have the eyes of a cat, this Luke Casement did. Dark as it was, he located her gripsacks and reached for them.

"Where's the rest of your luggage?"

"There is no more," she told him curtly. "For the length of time I expect to be here, I've all the luggage I need. And if you'll kindly return those bags, I'll—"

"We're wasting time," he cut in as though he hadn't even listened. But he had, for he added, "If you've qualms about my intentions, forget them. I'm trying to do you a favor. Also and besides, I'm reasonably civilized. So quit acting foolish and come along!"

He started off, and exasperated and reluctant

9

as she was, there was nothing for Sherry to do but follow. The way led past a sprawl of corrals and loading chutes where raw, dank odors told of recent bovine occupancy. Beyond the corrals, they had to cross some hundred yards of empty interval before the loom of buildings and a ragged scatter of lights marked the edge of the town proper. Here, as they turned into the run of a single street, a voice came out of the shadows.

"That the girl you been waitin' for, Luke?"

"She's the one, Gabe," Casement answered.

"Hah! Mebbe our luck's changin'. See you fill her ear with common sense before Francis Quinnault gets hold of her. And you—heads up, boy! For Cass Dutcher's in town. He's after Joe Moss again, raw-hidin' him shameful. Like he was talkin' to a dog, instead of a man. And he's served notice to Joe. Gave him until sunup tomorrow to clear plumb off this range."

"Cass Dutcher," said Casement tersely, "is pushing his luck. So is Milo Hernaman. One fine day the sky will fall on that pair. You get on back to headquarters, Gabe. See that Jack McCord's old room is cleaned up and ready. Miss Gault will likely be staying at the ranch starting tomorrow."

Increasingly aghast at what she was listening to, Sherry did not know whether to contain her growing exasperation at this continued calm taking over of her affairs or to explode in indignant anger

10

and give this Luke Casement a real dressing down. Before she could decide, the night turned wild with stunning abruptness.

Up the street a yell erupted. It was one of raging defiance, the cry of a human harassed and driven beyond all endurance. It carried a note of mad desperation that made Sherry's flesh crawl. It tapered off into shouted, challenging words.

"Hell with you, Dutcher! You hear me—hell with you! You don't run me off my range; you don't run me out of town. You think you can —come make your try. You hear me, Dutcher? Come on, you damned thievin' renegade! Make your try!"

From the dark, it was now Gabe to exclaim again.

"That's Moss—Joe Moss—callin' Dutcher out! Ah, the fool—the poor, brave fool! Luke, he won't stand a chance. Not against such as Dutcher. And this is what Dutcher's been aimin' at—an excuse to gun him down!"

All along the street movement was a bursting rush as men scurried about. Doors slammed. Voices called back and forth, then went into a quick stillness as a lift of high, sardonic, mocking words echoed to dominate and silence all the rest.

"All right, Moss! You want me—here I am!"

Strong hands caught hold of Sherry, swung her almost violently against the wall of a building,

11

and held her there behind the shield of Casement's shoulders.

Gunfire rolled out a hard, pounding racket. A man's shout lifted, then broke off into a choked cry of mortal hurt. Another shot blared, after which the night held to a long, shocked moment of taut silence. This was broken by another rush of men as they gathered about a figure lying still and crumpled in a thin pool of light that touched the street.

". . . Joe Moss," came the call. "He's done for!"

Out of the shadow, Gabe let go his strangled anger. "It was murder—coldblooded, calculated murder!"

The hands that had caught and held Sherry so unceremoniously now lifted her away from the building and into the clear again, where her charged-up resentment broke in full flood. For she was rumpled and confused, tired and frightened, burning with indignation.

She took her feelings out on Casement.

"Let go of me!" she stormed. "Don't ever touch me again! Do you understand? Don't touch me! Just—just leave me alone! I don't need you—or anyone else to tell me what to do, where to go! . . . Get away from me! You've no reason—no right—no—!"

"Easy does it!" He broke in on her outburst with some sternness. "You're not hurt, which is

12

the main thing. If your dignity is a little ruffled, it still isn't damaged beyond repair. If you're upset by the way I handled you, I'm sorry. But I had no time to explain why. Only—stray lead is no respecter of persons; it's been known to hit the innocent bystander before this. Also, out there —driven to frenzy by threats and ridicule and persecution—a poor desperate devil just died."

The harsh reality of this flat statement broke through Sherry's near tearful concern over her own small miseries. She gulped and stammered, "That—that shooting . . . you mean a man was . . . really killed?"

"Just so. Joe Moss—who never harmed anyone. But like you, he owned something Milo Hernaman has been wanting. So now he's dead, hounded into a showdown where he had no chance." The words rang with bitterness. Casement shook his head as though he could free it from the tentacles of punishing thought. He gathered the handles of the gripsacks in one big hand and took hold of her arm with the other, his touch gentle but iron hard. "That's the Humboldt House up there ahead."

It was a square, double-storied structure frowning down on the lesser buildings beside it. Across the upper-story front the windows were dark, blank eyes, but those of the lower level and the doorway they flanked beckoned with a warm inner glow.

13

Luke Casement brought Sherry Gault up the low steps of the long, deep porch. Here several men made a shadowy group, and Sherry felt their wondering glances. One of them spoke, his voice wet and heavy.

"Too bad—that business out there, Luke."

"It's what Hernaman and Dutcher have been wanting, isn't it?" returned Casement bleakly. "What are you going to do about it, Broady?"

"Moss asked for it." A note of sulky bluster showed in the heavy voice. "He called Dutcher out. He should have known better. It was an even shake. So what would you expect me to do?"

"Nothing. Not a damn thing, of course." Casement's contempt was open and cutting.

He guided Sherry through the hotel doorway. Here was a square, high-walled lobby, with hanging lamps sending down their spreading cones of radiance. There was a stairway climbing the rear wall, and at a register desk set under the angle of this, two women stood. One was gaunt and angular, gray of hair, with kindly eyes behind a pair of steel-rimmed spectacles. The other was about Sherry's age, in her mid-twenties. She made a long-legged, boyish figure in a divided skirt of faded blue denim, an open-throated tan cotton blouse, and an equally faded denim jumper. Under a mop of casually neat brown hair her face— though it was a trifle too broad for real beauty— was definitely attractive because of the agile mind and outright personality that shone through it.

14

Both of the women gave Sherry a shrewd feminine scrutiny as Casement brought her forward to make the introductions, naming the older one Mrs. Megarry, and the younger Katherine Larkin.

"Miss Gault," he explained, "is just off the *Limited* and hasn't seen much of good in our land so far. She'll be staying the night with you, Mrs. Megarry. Do your best by her." To Katherine Larkin he added, "How are things, Kate?"

"Rotten!" The reply was swift and pungent. "Luke, when is something going to be done about that foul brute Cass Dutcher? What's the matter with Broady Ives? Why doesn't he do something?"

"Because he's a politician, and a cheap one, before he is a law officer," Casement explained with blunt sarcasm. "Broady the politician plays his cards on the side where he thinks he sees the power. With Jack McCord out of the picture, he now sees it with Hernaman."

He turned back to Sherry. "Mrs. Megarry runs the best hotel and the best table in the state of Nevada, bar none. She'll treat you royal. And later on, when you feel up to some supper, I'll be around for that talk."

Upset as she had been out there in the blackness of the street with gun echoes rolling and a man dying, now that she was safe in warming light, with four walls to shut out the violence of the night and the comforting reassurance of someone of her own sex close at hand, some of the tumult abated. At least enough to allow her to appraise this man Luke Casement more clearly.

She had known he was tall from the moment he stepped out of the deeper darkness by the railroad tracks to take abrupt charge of her affairs. Now she saw that his face was very brown, with cheekbones that were high and slightly prominent, which set his eyes deep. Rock-gray eyes, with outer corners puckered from looking down many long, sunlit distances, which gave to his glance a degree of penetrating intentness. He wore a faded blue calico shirt and use-bleached jeans. His shoulders were wide and flat, his chest deep. His flanks were nipped and compact. There was a look of hard, tempered leanness all through him.

Meeting his glance, Sherry felt the warmth of blood stealing through her cheeks, and this heightened her feeling of antagonism toward him while stirring up an impatience with herself. So for a moment, she did not answer. It could have become a somewhat uncomfortable moment had he not, with quick perception, made it easier for her.

"Just remember," he told her gently, "in here you're among friends." He turned away then and went out.

Mrs. Megarry took over, smiling at Sherry as she swung the register into position.

"Judging by my own feelings in such matters, if there is one thing a body craves after days of train travel, it is hot water and plenty of it. I'll see

16

you get all you need. And room four is the best in the house."

Sherry signed the register and followed Mrs. Megarry up the stairs. Number four was a front corner room, and Sherry waited at the door of it while Mrs. Megarry, moving with knowing ease, lighted a pair of small wall-bracket lamps and a larger one that stood on the table beside the bed.

A single quick glance proved the truth of Mrs. Megarry's promise. The room was comfortable and spotlessly clean. There was a varnished pine bureau with a starched white runner across the top and a sizable mirror hanging above it. A smaller corner stand held a white china pitcher, a glass, and a washbowl. In another corner was an easy chair. The floor was carpeted, with an oval braided rag rug beside the bed. Several colorful autumn landscape prints decorated the walls. Mrs. Megarry was plainly awaiting her guest's approval, and Sherry gave it generously.

"It's very nice, really much better than I expected. I'm sure I'll find it very comfortable."

Mrs. Megarry beamed. "Should you feel you need more covers, there are extra blankets in the bureau drawers. The tub is in there." She pointed to an inner door. "Now I'll go get Mary Tyee busy with the hot water. Supper won't be ready for a good three-quarters of an hour yet. That should give you plenty of time to clean up."

Sherry showed a hint of stiffness. "I'm not too sure I'll be down for supper. I'm very tired."

"Not down for supper!" Mrs. Megarry exclaimed in disbelief. "Land sakes, child—of course, you'll be down. A body must eat. Besides, remember what Luke Casement said. He'll be expecting you."

She hurried away.

Sherry put her gripsacks by the bureau. "That's just it," she fumed crossly. "He'll be there. And everybody, it seems, stands ready to tell me my business! . . ."

She took off her hat and coat and tossed them on the bed. She crossed to the easy chair and sank into it, pushing back a fold of hair with weary fingers. So this was Battle Mountain—this was the storied wild West!

Well, she decided ruefully, so far it had more than lived up to the rougher aspects of its reputation, unreal as the night's savage incident now seemed. Sitting here in this comfortable, cheerfully lighted room it was hard to accept the reality that a man had died violently in front of a flaming gun within short yards of her.

As she had on the train, she wondered anew at her presence here. What wayward impulse had caused her to leave a well-paying position as a rising young dress designer in one of the swankiest shops on New York's Fifth Avenue and head for this particular spot in a sagebrush desert town to conclude the sale of a cattle ranch she had never known existed, let alone become the owner of?

The ranch had been left her by her mother's brother, an uncle she had seen but once in her life, so many years ago that she could barely recall him. She remembered him only as a big man with a great roaring voice and a violent presence. He had terrified her and upset the sedate little New England village where she and her mother lived, until everyone—her mother included—had known relief when he shouted his goodbyes and headed back to his favorite wilds.

No one could possibly have been more surprised than she on receiving a letter from an attorney in a Nevada town called Battle Mountain, notifying her of the inheritance. The attorney had signed himself Francis Quinnault. After congratulating her somewhat effusively on her good fortune, he had added further that should she so desire, he stood ready to sell the property for her. He had a responsible buyer available who was offering a price that was fair and generous, and he could conclude the transaction immediately on receipt of her written authority to do so. By postscript he added his recommendation that she accept the proposition without too much delay, since there was always the possibility that the prospective purchaser would change his mind. He plainly inferred that he hoped for a swift decision on her part.

It would have been easy to have followed Francis Quinnault's advice and conclude the whole affair by mail, and she had come close to doing so.

But at the last moment a wayward quirk of decision had cropped up. It could have been mere business acumen cautioning her to see for herself before selling, so that she might bargain more intelligently. Again, perhaps it had been a stir of conscience telling her that the right thing to do was at least to have a look at the property before disposing of it, that she owed at least this much to the generosity of a near-forgotten uncle who had not forgotten her.

Whatever the reason, here she was in a hotel room in Battle Mountain, while out there somewhere in the far miles of the night lay what Francis Quinnault had referred to as the Clear Creek Ranch, once the holdings of one John (Jack) McCord, but now her property through inheritance.

Tomorrow, she decided, she would hire transportation out to the ranch so that she might look at it and thus fulfill her obligation to the man who had left it to her. Afterward she would see the lawyer Francis Quinnault, meet with the prospective purchaser, arrive at a satisfactory settlement, and head back to her proper and desired groove in life to renew her interrupted career.

Beyond her door a step sounded, followed by a gentle knock. Sherry crossed and opened it.

Mary Tyee was a short, sturdy Shoshone Indian girl. She had brought two big buckets of steaming water. She showed Sherry a shy glance out of quick, dark eyes before lugging her burden to the inner door and opening it with a thrust of her strong young shoulder. Here, in the half-light thrown by the bedroom lamps, she emptied her buckets into the waiting tub.

"I bring you more," she told Sherry in tones softly guttural.

To Sherry the next half hour seemed about the most luxurious she had ever known. To be thoroughly warm and clean again, with much of her weariness and irritation washed away along with the grit and grime of travel! Now, also, such foolishness as not going down to supper was quickly forgotten. For as she stood before the mirror, working with the black luxury of her hair, she realized she was ravenously hungry.

What if Luke Casement was down there, waiting for her? She'd eat with him and listen to what he had to say. In all fairness she owed him something for his concern, even if it had been overbearing and frustrating. Yes, she'd let him have his talk, after which she would put him in his place—with emphasis! She'd let him know, very definitely, that he was through ordering her every move. . . .

Satisfied that she looked her best under the conditions, she gave her hair a final pat and prepared to leave. On casual impulse she hesitated, crossed to a window, and pulled aside the shade for a look at the street below.

It was a ribbon of blackness, cut irregularly

21

along its edges by ragged flares of reflected light. The shapes of men shifting here and there along it were dim, elusive images, beings of substance one moment, then vanishing as shadows as they moved from light to dark.

Through the closed window lifted the echoing ruffle of running hooves. A group of riders fled along the street and swung to a plunging halt before a saloon whose lights were the strongest and most garish of any Sherry could see. One of the riders called, and from somewhere a man answered. High, hard laughter rang, and the saloon door swung as the newly arrived group pushed through.

A wild street, thought Sherry. Night or day, a wild street whereon the rougher spirits of men roistered and fought, where men could—and did —die violently.

Of a sudden, in a splinter of light directly below her window, a man appeared. He wore a big white Stetson, and his upturned face was a dimly reflected blur. He had glimpsed Sherry and was staring up at her.

Quickly she stepped back, letting the shade swing into place. A stir of revulsion rippled through her, her feeling one of privacy spied upon.

Chapter TWO

THE DINING ROOM of the Humboldt House was a well-lighted area with a large central table and several smaller ones ranged along the walls. A scatter of diners was already present when Sherry Gault entered, and here again she felt the impact of a guarded scrutiny. At one of the smaller tables, Luke Casement sat with Katherine Larkin in some sort of quiet discussion. At Sherry's entrance Casement rose and came toward her. Katherine Larkin, still in her workaday denim clothes, flashed Sherry a quick glance then threaded past the tables into the kitchen beyond.

Sherry's manner was cool as she faced Casement. "If I'm intruding . . . ?"

"Not at all. Kate and I were just making ranch talk while waiting for you to show."

He held a chair for her, then took an opposite one. Mrs. Megarry appeared with a tray of food and beamed down on both of them. The food was savory, and Sherry's appetite was young and vigorous. She ate for a time in silence.

Presently her glance lifted. "You wished a talk. Very well—I'm prepared to listen."

Casement had shaved since she last saw him,

and the points of his high cheekbones shone coppery under the lights.

"First things first," he began slowly. "It is true that you intend selling the Clear Creek Ranch holdings to Milo Hernaman?"

Sherry nodded. "That is my intention. To sell the ranch, I mean. And while I have no idea who Milo Hernaman is, he could be a prospective buyer."

"The one Francis Quinnault suggested?"

"Possibly. Though Mr. Quinnault named no one definitely. He merely informed me by mail that he had a buyer lined up. And for some reason you apparently disapprove. Though why you should feel any concern in the matter, I can't imagine."

"I have my reasons. I hope to show you enough of them to persuade you not to sell. Not to sell to anybody—least of all Milo Hernaman."

"In that case," Sherry told him flatly, "you are wasting both your time and mine. As I have definitely decided to get rid of the property."

Casement studied her with his gray, penetrating glance. "Why? It's a good ranch—a very good ranch, one of the best. It represents a man's lifetime of work, sacrifice, and hardship. And if Jack McCord had even dreamed such a damned scavenging pirate as Milo Hernaman might someday own all he'd slaved and—yes, bled for a time or two—he'd have destroyed it with his own hands before he died."

24

Sherry flushed under the pressing intensity of his tone. "You speak of reasons why I shouldn't sell. Well, I have some of my own why I should—and will. To me they are very legitimate reasons. To begin with, I've no slightest idea how to run a ranch, nor do I wish to learn how. This may be your kind of country, but it isn't mine. To you, this Clear Creek Ranch may be many things. To me it is only a means to an end. Sale of it will enable me to further my own desired career among surroundings I prefer to live in. Those surroundings are certainly not a cattle ranch in country like this. So, whatever you may think of them, my reasons suit me."

Casement scrubbed a restless hand across his face. "How about the little ranchers living side by side with Clear Creek? To them the ranch has meant security, because Jack McCord made the outfit big and strong enough to be a power in the county. He protected the little ranchers who were his neighbors. He respected their rights and they respected his. They were his friends. When he died they gathered to help bury him. They mourned him then—they mourn him now. But if Milo Hernaman ever gets his hands on the Clear Creek Ranch, those little ranchers—Jack McCord's friends—will be wiped out. Hernaman will run over them like a plague, hogging their range."

In spite of herself, Sherry could not completely ignore the fervor in the words of this lean, brown-faced man. "Wiped out—overrun? I don't understand. How could this—this Milo Hernaman do these things?"

Casement shrugged. "There's no limit to the greed of the man or to his hunger to dominate and possess—or the limits he'll go to to get what he wants. Consider Joe Moss, gunned down in the street hardly more than an hour ago. Doesn't seem real, does it? But it was—too damned real! And why? Well, Joe had something Hernaman wanted—a little chunk of range that fitted into Hernaman's plans because it adjoins a portion of Clear Creek range. Getting it, Hernaman has a foothold from which to edge in on Clear Creek. And this, above all else, is what Hernaman wants most of all, Clear Creek Ranch—that's it. Once he has it, he'll also have this whole county by the throat."

Casement paused, his words running out into a moment of dark, bitter brooding. He shrugged again. "Yes, it was Joe Moss's misfortune to own something Hernaman wanted. Oh, Hernaman first tried to buy it—but at his own price, you understand—a price that was sheer robbery. Naturally, Joe turned him down. Now Joe is dead. And within a week Dollar cattle—the dollar sign is Milo Hernaman's brand, as well as his god—will be grazing on that piece of range."

"You speak of things that to me—well, just don't seem possible," Sherry declared, trying to hide a rising stir of uncertainty. "After all, there

26

is such a thing as law. If this Milo Hernaman killed a man, he should answer to the authorities."

Casement laughed. It was short and mirthless. "What authorities? Broady Ives is supposed to be such in these parts. Supposed to be, that's all. And of course Hernaman was not in on the actual shooting. He had his pet gun-dog, Cass Dutcher, handle that chore. Dutcher did it by whipsawing Joe Moss until, unable to take it any longer, Joe called him out. That allowed Broady Ives to name it an even break, with Moss the aggressor, which leaves Dutcher—and Hernaman—in the clear. Though everybody knows Joe Moss didn't stand a chance in the gunplay—not against such as Dutcher. Oh, it's not a pretty picture, but I've given you the facts."

Sherry went silent for a little time, picking at her food somewhat aimlessly. When she finally spoke it was slowly, selecting each word with care. "Please believe me when I say that in selling the ranch I have no wish to hurt anyone in any way. Yet what else can I do? My home—my life, the kind of existence I know and desire—is far away from here. As I said before, I know absolutely nothing about ranching or—or raising cattle. Don't you see, Mr. Casement—being who I am and what I am, there is nothing I can reasonably be expected to do but dispose of the property to my best advantage. Don't you see?"

By the time she finished, the wall of hostility she had tried to maintain against him fell apart completely. She was suddenly appealingly young and uncertain, and Casement saw her so.

His expression softened. "I understand," he agreed quietly. "My line of thought hasn't been very realistic. Some pretty capable men have attempted to stand against Milo Hernaman and his damned empire of greed, without making a dent in it. And here I've been trying to talk you into trying where they failed."

She responded to his change of mood. "You feel very strongly about it, don't you?"

Casement nodded soberly. "I worked for Jack McCord. I know what the ranch meant to him and to a lot of other people. I know what went into the building of it and what could come out of it. And when you've helped build something, you hate to think of it being torn apart."

"When I sell, would it help if I refused to consider any offer from this—this Milo Hernaman?" Sherry queried.

Casement showed a small, twisted smile. "If you sell at all, you'll sell to Hernaman. I know of nobody who is in a position to buck him or who could come up with enough money."

Sherry straightened in her chair. "You make it sound as if Clear Creek Ranch was a small kingdom."

Casement's glance turned sharp with a quick interest. "Did Francis Quinnault tell you how much Hernaman offered?"

"Wh-why yes, he did. He mentioned the offer

when he notified me that he had a prospective buyer."

"If," asserted Casement tersely, "it was less than a hundred thousand, it would amount to highway robbery."

Sherry's eyes went wide and she caught her breath. "A hundred thousand! Surely you're wrong. You can't mean that!"

"Rock bottom," Casement insisted. "What was Hernaman ready to deal for—about fifteen?"

"How—how did you guess? It was—exactly fifteen thousand. It seemed a great deal of money to me."

Casement's smile was small and mirthless again as he shook his head musingly.

"Fifteen thousand. What a steal that would have been! But that's Hernaman for you. Once I worked for him. Back when I was a bald-faced kid not old enough to have good sense, I signed on with Hernaman. It took me just one month to get all I wanted of him." Casement shook his head again. "Fifteen thousand dollars! As a willing partner to such a fraud, Francis Quinnault has sunk lower than I thought."

Sherry tried to put her thoughts in order. From the moment of reading Francis Quinnault's letter advising her of her inheritance and what it could be sold for, she had visualized the sum and all the things she might do with it. Fifteen thousand dollars! Why she might even have opened a dress shop of her own. Yet, fifteen thousand was almost nothing, compared with what Luke Casement was telling her the ranch was really worth!

"I don't know what to think; I don't know what to say," she admitted somewhat breathlessly. "And I don't know what to do."

"One thing you certainly should do," Casement said. "You should have a good look at the ranch before you sell it. I'd be glad to drive you out there tomorrow."

She hesitated before nodding slowly. "Very well. I had really decided to visit the ranch before closing the sale of it. I felt I owed that much to the memory of my uncle."

"I'll have a rig ready first thing in the morning," Casement promised. "And don't you agree to anything with anybody, or sign anything, until you've seen Clear Creek. A bargain?"

He was leaning forward, quick eagerness in his face. She studied him for a sober moment. Until this moment he had seemed a man who, though right by you, talking to you, looking at you, stood at the fringe of a remoteness where you could not touch him. Now he was somehow easier to know, to talk to.

"A bargain," Sherry said, and smiled.

"Clever girl!" He glanced past her and lowered his voice to a warning murmur. "Prepare to resist the blandishments of an overdone fountain of lofty oratory. None other than Francis Quinnault approaches!"

Startled, Sherry looked up as a man stopped beside the table. Luke Casement got to his feet. "Evening, Quinnault!" he drawled. "It appears an introduction is in order. Meet Miss Sherry Gault. I'll leave her in your care. See you don't abuse the confidence. And, Quinnault—you should brush up on your figures and learn to count higher than fifteen." He looked at Sherry again. "Until tomorrow, then?"

She nodded. "Until tomorrow." On impulse she added. "And thank you for everything."

She watched him walk away. A diner at the long center table neglected a busy plate to say something to him. Casement dropped a hand on the speaker's shoulder as he gave answer, the lean hard lines of his face breaking into a quick smile. Then he went on, a tall man who moved with a lithe, sure ease.

Sherry turned her glance to Francis Quinnault and saw that he also had watched Casement leave. Now, meeting her glance, the lawyer shrugged his sharp shoulders.

"Unpredictable, that fellow Casement is. Given to rather strange statements. I might even class him as one of our more intractable citizens. I never was able to understand John McCord's thinking in keeping him on as foreman and riding boss. But that is aside from the pleasure of the moment, Miss Gault. May I have a cup of coffee with you?"

31

Without waiting for an answer, Quinnault took the chair Luke Casement had just vacated. Sherry studied him curiously.

He was very thin, and his clothes hung on him loosely. A roach of ragged, slightly yellowed hair flared back over his head, and a moustache and goatee of the same drab shade shrouded the tight, thin line of his lips and his narrow, pointed chin. Under bushy brows his eyes were brown and shiny as flecks of bottle glass. His cheeks were sallow and whiskey veined. He reminded her somewhat of a flamboyant, down-at-the-heels Shakespearian actor. She was wondering what to say to him, when Mrs. Megarry came by and saved the moment.

"Just a cup of coffee if you please, madam," Quinnault ordered.

Mrs. Megarry sniffed. " 'Twould do you good, Francis Quinnault, to drink less and eat more. Which I have told you before." She went off to fetch the coffee.

The lawyer shook his head. "An admirable woman, Mrs. Megarry. But one who does not understand all the needs of a man. Ah—Miss Gault, you have considered the offer I mentioned in our correspondence."

"Yes," Sherry told him carefully. "Yes, I have."

"Good! You are prepared to act on it?"

"Not immediately." Sherry continued her careful selection of words. "Before I decide on anything I am having a look at the property."

Francis Quinnault's goatee bristled importantly.

"I must emphasize, Miss Gault, that time is a factor in this matter. The buyer I have in mind is a busy man, with many wide business interests. If kept waiting too long, he could—as I so stated in my letter to you—very well change his mind."

"I don't believe you have yet mentioned the name of this buyer, Mr. Quinnault," Sherry reminded. "Would it be a man named Hernaman—Milo Hernaman?"

Francis Quinnault blinked. "Why—why, yes —it is Mr. Hernaman. And as I say, a busy man— a very busy—"

"Then we must find another buyer," Sherry cut in. "Because I do not intend to sell to Milo Hernaman or anyone else at the first price offered."

Some of Francis Quinnault's initial heartiness dried up. "That might be difficult to arrange. Locating a second possible buyer, I mean. At the moment I know of no one other than Mr. Hernaman who is interested. And even with Mr. Hernaman I must state again how important the question of time is. I feel we should move quickly, Miss Gault."

"There are," returned Sherry with some tartness, "times to move quickly and times not to. This is one not to. We will move slowly and make a real effort to find another interested buyer besides this Milo Hernaman. That is the way I wish it."

Mrs. Megarry came and put Francis Quinnault's coffee in front of him. It was steaming hot; yet he gulped it somewhat avidly, not entirely able to hide his expression of dismay behind the tilted cup. He seemed momentarily at a loss for words.

"Very well," he managed finally, putting the cup down. "I will see what I can do about another buyer. Though I cannot promise anything too quickly."

Sherry pushed back her chair. "I have time to wait. You can let me know when something turns up. Now, if you'll excuse me . . ." She moved out into the hotel lobby, a slender, graceful figure.

Francis Quinnault remained as he was for a little time, staring straight ahead with a bleak, unreadable gaze. Then he rose and left, moving quickly through the foyer and out into the night. He turned along the street to the door of a darkened office and pushed through it.

In the room he entered, cigar smoke laid an invisible thickness, and the faintest reach of light from the street reflected on a big white Stetson. The owner of the hat made inquiry with a brief, heavy arrogance. "Well?"

"She's playing coy," reported Quinnault. "Flatly rejects our offer. Insists that another buyer be located. Also refuses to be rushed. Finally, she intends having a look at the ranch before she does anything."

"She's smarter than we figured," growled Milo Hernaman, pushing his big white hat back with

34

an irritated gesture. "Either that or somebody has been advising her."

"Casement, no doubt," Quinnault stated acidly. "He was sitting with her at supper when I went in."

"There's one who's been around too long," Hernaman said harshly. "And tonight is as good a time as any to do something about that. Cass Dutcher will be over at the Enterprise. Go get him and bring him here."

Francis Quinnault did not immediately obey. "Sure that's wise?" he asked carefully.

"What do you mean?" demanded Hernaman.

"Well, there's the Joe Moss business," Quinnault said. "Here and there I've heard talk. Quite a few people liked Joe Moss. Those same people don't like Cass Dutcher. Don't you see where the trail leads after it gets past Dutcher? I'd say the town has had about all the rough play for one evening it can take. And Luke Casement is a lot bigger man in the public eye than Joe Moss was. Maybe it would be smart to go after Casement some other way, some other time."

"Hell with what the public thinks!" Hernaman snapped. "And I can't afford to wait for a better time. Go get Dutcher."

When Francis Quinnault left the Humboldt House, Sherry Gault had been climbing the stairs out of the lobby. Watching him, she noted a vague furtiveness in his manner, and her feeling of con-

35

cern deepened. You could, she decided wearily, inherit more than mere money or property. You could also inherit trouble. . . .

On going to supper she had left the lights burning in her room and had also closed the door. Now the door stood open, and as she stepped through it, wondering, Kate Larkin spoke from the room's easy chair.

"I hope you won't mind my taking over like this. But since we might have reason to let our hair down a little, I thought it best we do it here instead of in the lobby."

Once more was Sherry faced with the forthright almost abrupt manner of this Western land. She was finding it difficult to adjust to. She stiffened. "Really—I don't—well . . ."

"Now, now," soothed her visitor easily. "Don't jump over the traces. As Luke Casement told you—with him or me, you're among friends. We both wish you nothing but good. Actually, in owning Clear Creek Ranch, you're a next-door neighbor of mine. So ease down while we swap a few opinions."

Sherry crossed to the bed and sat on the edge of it. "Opinions—or advice? I've heard a lot about Western hospitality, which apparently also includes a great deal of advice on one's personal affairs."

"You shouldn't use sarcasm, my dear," retorted Kate Larkin bluntly. "It doesn't become you. You are entirely too nice a person to deal with it.

36

You are also the original babe in the woods where Clear Creek Ranch affairs are concerned, especially when you deal with such as Francis Quinnault and Milo Hernaman. There, you can use plenty of advice."

Innate honesty asserted itself. "I'm sorry," Sherry said contritely. "You're right—I do need advice. So far, I've seen very little of Francis Quinnault, but it has been enough to make me wonder at my uncle's leaving things in such hands."

"You didn't know Jack McCord very well, did you?"

Sherry shook her head. "I saw him but once in my life, back when I was a small child. I hardly remember him. I retain a dim impression of a great, roaring, violent man."

"He was a big man," Kate Larkin said. "Big in many ways. In his friendships, in his hates; in his virtues and his faults. In his trusts, too, which was his greatest weakness. His friends would have died for him, but some men he trusted too much. Francis Quinnault was one of them. In fact, if Jack McCord's will had not been on official record, you might never have heard of any inheritance. As it was, Quinnault had no other out but to notify you. But now, should you let him, he'd cheat you out of your eyeteeth."

Sherry smiled faintly. "You put it plainly enough."

"Why not, when it is a fact?" declared Kate Larkin. "Quinnault is playing up to Milo Hernaman, now that he thinks Hernaman will be the big man in the county. So is that pompous, fumbling fool of a Broady Ives, who lets murder be done in the street and builds up a farfetched, hypocritical excuse for letting it stand."

"That is something else I find difficult to understand," Sherry said slowly. "How a man can be shot down in a public street before witnesses, and nothing be done about it. I—it was—rather terrible, wasn't it? The guns—the sound of them— and a man crying out in mortal hurt . . . !" She shivered slightly.

"Joe Moss was a neighbor of my brother and me," Kate Larkin said gravely. "One by one, Milo Hernaman finds ways to get rid of us. I'm wondering when our turn will come, as it surely will, once Hernaman gets Clear Creek Ranch. You intend to sell, of course?"

Bitterness crept into Kate Larkin's words. Sherry stirred under the bite of them.

"What else can I do?" she defended. "I can't run a ranch—I wouldn't know where or how to start. If I actually had to fight to retain my holdings, as some think could happen, what would I fight with—these?" She held up slender hands. "Call me a weak woman if you want, but I know of no way to benefit by my inheritance, other than to sell. Preferably not to this Milo Hernaman person, but to someone."

38

"You could," suggested Kate Larkin, "keep the ranch and let someone run it for you. Someone like Luke Casement. I know of no one better qualified."

Sherry shook her head again. "That arrangement would never work. With me in New York and the ranch out here, it would be too much of a long-distance affair."

For a little time Kate Larkin brooded, staring at nothing. Then she shrugged resignedly. "Don't mind me. You have a perfect right to do as you please with your ranch. And you owe none of us —" She broke off, listening.

It came up from the street, a sudden, hard, excited rumble of men's voices, increasing quickly in power and amount. Kate Larkin interpreted the sound instantly and was on her feet, crossing to the window.

"Dear God!" she exclaimed. "Not again! Who could it be now?"

She sent the shade whipping up, opened the window, and leaned out. The sound of the street was a jungle growl. Out of it a voice carried as before, the same high, taunting voice that had mocked Joe Moss to his death.

"All right, Casement! I want to know about this—about you makin' talk of other folks behind their backs, including me. Not very nice talk, either. I don't like that, Casement—I don't like it at all. Suppose you say it again—to my face. While I'm lookin' at you!"

Kate Larkin cried out softly. "No, Luke—no! Don't let him lead you into it! Luke—no!"

Sherry moved quickly to Kate Larkin's side, a coldness rolling through her. Down there the street was as she had seen it before going to supper, a canyon of mixed dark and reflected splinters of light, all astir with the doings of men. Wicked doings this time with human shadows bunched and crowding here and there, though staying well out of line of the two figures facing each other across the street's width, each outlined with fair clarity by the furtive light glow.

There was no mistaking the tall stillness of Luke Casement, and to Sherry, the other did not count.

Casement spoke, his words cold and distinct. "Playing it safe as usual, eh Dutcher? I've no gun on me, as you well know. If I had one, you wouldn't be out there making big talk and swagger. You'd be hiding in a hole somewhere."

Dutcher flared savagely. "Somebody give him a gun!"

"I don't want just any gun," Casement countered. "The gun I want is the one you used on Joe Moss. You carry that one and a mate to it. Maybe you figure you need two against an unarmed man?"

A rumble went through the crowd. "How about that, Dutcher?" someone called. "You want action—give him one of your guns."

Cass Dutcher was a lank, malignant figure there at the edge of darkness and light. He was a man without a friend in the street, and he knew it. Individually and collectively they hated him and feared him for what he was. Under the protection of darkness the heckler spurred him again.

"What's the matter, Dutcher—you shoot all your birds on the sit? Or maybe you like 'em handier with a skillet than with a gun—like it was with Joe Moss?"

It caught on with the crowd, and a sweep of jeering began.

Down the corridor of several wicked years, Cass Dutcher had fashioned a vicious, deadly reputation for himself. To maintain it now, there was nothing he could do but move out toward the center of the street.

"Come get that gun, Casement. You want it— come get it!"

Luke Casement moved to meet him, and Kate Larkin gave a smothered, almost sobbing cry. Sherry Gault, standing beside her, put an arm about her and held her tightly, wordless and frozen herself.

It seemed that even in the tricky gloom of the street Sherry had never seen anything that stood out with such clarity as those two stalking, steadily nearing figures down there. Step by step the interval closed until a bare two yards separated the pair. Dutcher drew a gun and tossed it at Casement's feet.

"There's the one you asked for, Casement. Pick it up!"

"Why sure," Casement drawled. "Sure—!"

He leaned, as though to reach for the weapon, then, from this half crouch, with his feet gathered and set beneath him for leverage, went into Dutcher with a driving, explosive lunge, his hunched shoulder smashing into the gunman just ahead of the fellow's attempt to draw his second weapon. The impact threw Dutcher reeling off balance. Before he could recover, a winging, vengeful fist ripped home to his jaw, knocking him back and down.

Casement was on him, panther-fast, grabbing at that near-drawn gun, tearing it out of Dutcher's half-stunned grasp and throwing it aside.

"Now!" he charged harshly. "Now, Dutcher —you get it!"

A man in the crowd whooped wildly. "You got him, Luke—you got him! Stomp him! Bust him up! You got him—finish him!"

"In my own way," Casement pronounced coldly. "Tonight, Dutcher doesn't ride out of town. Tonight, he crawls out. On his hands and knees. You hear that, Dutcher? Tonight you crawl! This, Dutcher—is for Joe Moss!"

Sherry Gault missed no word, no move. She saw Casement haul Dutcher upright, then smash him down again. She saw him do this twice and a third time, while the pushing, swaying, exulting crowd howled its approval with the throaty savagery of wolves.

She had never witnessed anything like it before. It was pitiless, it was brutal, it was cruel. She wanted to turn away, to close her eyes and ears, but she couldn't. She was held by a fascination she could neither understand nor break.

A fourth time Casement hauled his man erect, only to hammer him down again with another coldly calculated, punishing blow. And the words came echoing—bleak, remorseless. "It can go on all night, Dutcher—until you crawl!"

So, presently, punished into a half-blind fear, Cass Dutcher crawled. A lank, near-stunned and savagely beaten figure dragging along on hands and knees through the trampled dust of the street. The crowd, jeering and whooping exultantly, closed in until Luke Casement and the man he had beaten down to the semblance of a whipped animal were hidden in the dark center of the jostling mass.

Now at last Sherry was able to turn away, hands pressed to her face. "Jungle beasts!" she choked. "Brutes—barbarians! All of them—not even half-human . . . !"

"Stop it!" Kate Larkin faced her, flaring. "You don't know what you're saying!" The shine of tears was in Kate's eyes, tears of fiery pride. "For you just watched a brave man give this town back a little of its self-respect. Yes, you just watched

43

Luke Casement do that!" Kate hurried out and down the stairs.

Sherry closed her door and locked it. Abruptly she was lonely, forlorn—half-sick with upsetting emotions. Deepening chill came in at the open window. She put out the lights, undressed quickly in the dark, and climbed into bed. She lay there hating the town, hating the country, even hating the people—and so homesick for safe, familiar scenes and surroundings that she wept a little.

Done presently with tears, she vowed fiercely that on the morrow she would complete quickly what she had come west to do. She would close out the sale of the ranch, accept the sum Francis Quinnault had offered, then catch the next eastbound *Overland Limited* and head for home as fast as speeding wheels could get her there.

But the bed was soft and warm, so presently she relaxed. The town was now reasonably quiet again, with the echo of men's voices lifting from the street in calmer, more scattered tones. These too gradually frittered out, and night's great, elemental stillness settled solidly down.

A small wind filtered in through the open window. On it rode the dry-sweet incense of cedar and sage and the aromatic pungency of juniper. At some great distance a coyote yodeled at the stars.

On this wild note, Sherry Gault slept.

44

Chapter THREE

THE GLITTER of early-morning sunlight slanted in at the open window. From the street below, stirred by the bright face of this new day, someone lifted a cheerful whistling. From beyond the freight yards the strident cry of a freight engine sailed across the house tops of the town of Battle Mountain in a long, insistent banner of sound. Sherry Gault stirred sleepily, reluctant to leave the warm cocoon of her blankets.

There came a light tapping at the door. Sherry stirred again and answered drowsily, "Yes—what is it?"

"Coffee for you." The words came in Mary Tyee's guttural tone.

Sherry threw aside the blankets and straightened, stretching widespread arms and yawning luxuriously. She stifled the yawn with the back of her hand, donned a light robe, and unlocked the door.

Crossing quickly to put the morning cup on the table by the bed, the Indian girl smiled her shy greeting. Just as swiftly she retreated, pausing only for one further announcement before closing the door behind her. "Breakfast waiting downstairs. You hurry."

Sherry perched on the edge of the bed and sipped her coffee. So breakfast was waiting. And please hurry. Just like that you were reminded, she thought crossly. In these parts you could not order your own time. The country had a pace of its own, and you were expected to answer to it even if you were a guest—and a paying one.

Well, she wouldn't put up with that sort of thing any longer than she absolutely had to. The final thought she had carried into sleep last night remained the first one in her mind now. Nor had the vow she had then made weakened in any way. What if Francis Quinnault was a shady character and the price he offered for the ranch on the light side? If it suited her, then it didn't have to suit anybody else. Besides, in all probability that man—that Luke Casement—had exaggerated wildly when he spoke of a hundred thousand dollars. How could some ratty old ranch in this ratty country possibly be worth that much money? Hadn't she looked out of a Pullman window at endless miles of such country and seen nothing but sagebrush? . . .

She drained the cup, then set about washing up in the heavy china bowl on the stand. The water she poured from the pitcher was icy, and the touch of it made her cringe. But it quite definitely washed away the last dregs of sleepiness and put roses in her cheeks, as she noted when she stood

46

before the mirror to dress and to put up her hair.

In spite of the antagonism she had managed to amass within herself toward this desert country with its people and its ways, she had to admit to a definite sense of physical well-being and buoyancy as she dropped down the stairs to the Humboldt House lobby and in turn from there into the dining room. Whether this was because of the reviving influence of a good night's sleep and the vitalizing lift of the thin, keen air—or merely anticipation of breakfast—she did not know. At any rate it was there, and strongly so.

It was strong enough even to withstand a small stir of dismay at sight of Luke Casement sitting at a far corner table. What with last night's memory of his deliberately beating another human being down to the status of a crawling animal still raw and repugnant before her, he was the last person she wanted to see. There was, however, no escaping him as he stood to greet her.

Eyeing her steadily, he read something of her thoughts and mood. "That," he said quietly, "was then. This is now. And all of it will look a lot different to you in a few days."

He held her chair for her, and there was nothing she could do about that, either. But when he resumed his seat she spoke with a cold directness. "I won't be anywhere near here in a few days if I can help it. I'll be back home, or on my way there. I am withdrawing my promise to ride out to Clear Creek with you. I think you understand why."

47

"No," Casement said. "I don't understand why."

"Not after that beastly affair you were in last night?"

"No, not even after that, for I can't see why it should interfere in any way with the handling of your ranch inheritance in a common-sense deal. So you watched last night's affair, then?"

"All of it. From my window. It was disgusting, revolting, horrible. And—and that awful crowd of men, howling like mad animals! What kind of people live out here?"

"Basically the same kind as where you came from—some good, some bad. Happily, there are more of the good ones than the other kind, else the world would really be a jungle." Pausing for a moment, Casement admitted, "The sort of thing you watched is never pretty. But when it is thrust at a man he has to face up to it in his own way."

"And your way was to beat another human down to something terrified and crawling? You'd try and justify that?"

Sherry's glance was as fiery as her words.

"Cass Dutcher," said Casement patiently, "was out to kill me, just as he did Joe Moss. And for the same reason, probably. An order from Milo Hernaman." The import behind the words turned them bleak. "What would you have had me do?"

"It might have been kinder if you'd taken the gun he threw at your feet—and used it on him.

48

Yes, that might have been kinder than—than destroying him the way you did."

Casement's smile was small and dry and devoid of any semblance of mirth. "At that particular moment I wasn't thinking in terms of kindness. Also, I'd have been thoroughly dead the second I touched the gun. It was what Dutcher was hoping for—that I'd make a grab at the gun and try for him. Had I done so he could have claimed an even break and self-defense as he shot me down. Oh, I can take care of myself with a gun pretty well, but not against such as Dutcher when he holds that big an edge. Besides, I'm a cattleman, not a gunfighter. So I let Dutcher think I was falling for his little game, then handled him in my own way. You say I should have killed him. Perhaps I have."

Sherry stared, her eyes widening. "You mean —you actually beat him to death? With your bare hands you—you actually . . . ?"

"Not literally," Casement cut in. "But a man like Dutcher has two weapons—his guns and the reputation he builds with them. The reputation can be almost as effective as the guns, so long as it holds. Once it's shattered, however, your gunfighter is disarmed by half. Men no longer fear him as they did, and the edge he once held because of that fear no longer exists. He has ceased to be the invincible killer. Then it is merely a matter of time before the law of the gun catches up

49

with him. Last night, when I made Cass Dutcher crawl, I destroyed the reputation—I smashed the image of fear. To that extent I killed him."

Before Sherry could find suitable retort to this, Mrs. Megarry appeared with an armful of steaming breakfast dishes. "What a fine, sweet morning this is!" she exclaimed with smiling cheer for them both. To Sherry she added, "I envy you the ride out to Clear Creek and the chance to see all of your ranch spreading rich and wonderful under God's great sky. You must be looking forward to it."

"On the contrary, I'm not," returned Sherry shortly. "Neither am I riding out to Clear Creek. All I'm looking forward to is settling my affairs with Francis Quinnault as quickly as possible so that I may head back where I belong."

Mrs. Megarry stiffened, her lips pursing sternly. A combative gleam quickened behind the steel rims of her spectacles. "That, my young missy, was not a thing well said. And if you mean it, then you simply don't care, more's the shame! It makes empty the thing Jack McCord held most dear. For I knew Jack McCord, and well—so well that had he spoken outright to me before Hollis Megarry came along, I might this moment stand as your lawful aunt. Yes, I knew Jack McCord when we were both young and had our great dreams in a world that was young and great too. I know the work and sweat and sacrifice that went into the building of Clear Creek Ranch and what it meant to the man who built it."

The lift of an imperative hand held Sherry to silence while Mrs. Megarry continued. "I was with Jack McCord the day he died, and he told me then how happy he was to have kin to leave his ranch to. He spoke of a slip of a black-haired little girl he had once seen long ago, one he would have liked to have held on his knee. But for some reason she seemed to fear him and would not get close to him. But he never forgot that little girl, who now, as a young woman grown, would inherit the ranch. So he died, and though among friends, yet was he lonely for his last known kin. Down all the years he had kept alive in his heart a love for the black-haired little girl who would not sit on his knee. Just to think of it puts a tear in my eye, so it does!"

Having had her say, Mrs. Megarry marched away, blinking rapidly.

Sherry did some blinking of her own. She also swallowed a little thickly. She fumbled for a handkerchief and dabbed at her eyes. "She—she had no right to say that. I—I didn't know my uncle felt so. I—had no idea. How—how could I have known?"

"You couldn't, of course," Casement comforted. "And Mrs. Megarry didn't mean to be unkind. It's just that she thought a lot of Jack McCord."

51

"She made it sound like I was horribly selfish—and self-centered. When I'm not at all like that—really I'm not." Sherry dabbed at her eyes again before adding a muffled admission. "Now I have to—to ride out to the ranch. Else I'd hate myself forever."

"That's the stuff! That squares everything. I've a rig and team waiting. Get on with your breakfast. You'll feel much better as soon as we get rolling."

Oddly enough, Sherry felt better almost immediately. Renewing her intention to go out to the ranch relieved an inner tension and rid her of an attitude that—though she was reluctant to admit it, even to herself—she had begun to regret. She started on her breakfast and found herself enjoying it fully.

Glancing at Casement she saw a hint of amusement in his eyes. She tossed her head. "Oh, I know you think I'm an awful ninny, saying a thing one moment and something just the opposite the next. Like—well, perhaps I didn't know my own mind."

"No, I wouldn't say that," Casement said mildly. "You've had a situation tossed in your lap which could confuse and upset someone far older and with considerably more experience with the world and its ways. Also, you've met up with a couple of angles hardly calculated to make the country and its ways more attractive to you. I think you're doing fine."

High on one cheek he carried an abrasion, and the knuckles of his right hand were swollen and bruised—visible reminders, Sherry knew, of the violent showdown in the street last night with Cass Dutcher. That affair now seemed as unreal to her as the Joe Moss shooting. After dressing and before coming down to breakfast, she had paused for a moment at her window to look down at the street. Last night it had been a dark canyon full of deadly fury and brute conflict; this morning it was just a dusty run of comparative emptiness lying peaceful in the quickening pour of the sun.

She found this was one of the disturbing aspects of this wide desert—these strong contrasts between its several faces. Nights could be deeply black and savage, and days could be clear and cheerful. And the people moved with easy acceptance of either mood. Perhaps that was because they lived closer to the fundamentals, to the unchangeable realities, be they dark or bright. Hence their thinking was less complicated and along straighter lines than that of their counterparts back home. Here was less pretense, less posturing, and sterner judgments. Here black was black and white was white, with no sickly gray in between sentiments trying to justify that which could not be justified. Here a thing simply was or was not. . . .

"Got it all figured?" Casement drawled, amusement in his voice as well as his eyes.

Sherry flushed, nodding a little sheepishly. "Some of it, perhaps."

"Life," observed Casement, "is only as complicated as you choose to make it. A fact is always a fact. Long as you remember that you're on the right trail."

Mrs. Megarry returned, ready to pour more coffee. Her kindly smile was working again. Sherry showed one of her own to match it.

"Thanks for the scolding, Mrs. Megarry. I had it coming. I'm riding out to the ranch after all."

Mrs. Megarry exclaimed, "Bless you, child! I knew you would, just as soon as you stopped to think about it. Maybe I better fix a lunch for you to take along?"

"You do, you'll have Gabe Tennant mad at you," warned Casement humorously. "He figures to have the fatted calf all laid out and waiting himself."

Mrs. Megarry sniffed. "That crusty old heathen! Is he so proud of his cooking then?"

Casement grinned. "He'll do to take along, Gabe will. He can do a pretty fair job of anything he sets his mind to."

Mrs. Megarry sniffed again as she turned away. "He'll likely choke someday on one of his own biscuits."

Casement's grin became a soft chuckle as Mrs. Megarry returned to her kitchen. "Always an argument when Mrs. Megarry and Gabe Tennant get together," he told Sherry. "Yet, back three or four years ago when Gabe broke a leg, she nursed him like a baby. And if anybody ever spoke a mean word of Maggie Megarry in Gabe's hearing, they'd get their ears torn off."

Sherry considered this remark, a musing half smile on her lips. Presently she nodded. "I think I'm beginning to understand you people out here. Just a little, I think I am."

Casement's rig was a buckboard drawn by a team of sorrels that were full of run. They left town with a rush that had Sherry hanging on to the iron seat rail with one hand and to her hat with the other. The road was a ribbon of dusty tawniness threading the far distance of blue-gray sage. The air flowing against her face was keen and redolent with the fine, clean flavors of space, and it stirred an unexpected exhilaration that parted her lips and put a shine in her eyes.

After the first fast couple of miles, the sorrels slowed to a pace that enabled Sherry to look around and take stock.

"Well!" she exclaimed, settling her hat more firmly on her head and tucking some tendrils of wind-loosened hair back into place. "That was what I'd call an experience. For a time I thought I was riding in a runaway."

Casement chuckled, flicking lightly at the working haunches of the team with the tip of his whip. "The broncs have been living high and lazy for the best part of a week at Jimmy Ink's livery stable. They were fretting to go, so I let 'em get it out of their systems. I held 'em back some. I didn't want to lose you if we happened to hit a real chuck hole."

"At this speed it shouldn't take long to get where we are going," Sherry suggested.

Casement pointed with his whip. "See that sad-dlebacked ridge way out there ahead? And out past the east end of it that other chunk of uplift with the flat top? Well, that yonder piece is part of the Clear Creek Rim. When we haul up right against that rim—right up under it—then we'll be home."

Sherry stared, somewhat aghast. "Why—why it looks miles and miles away."

"It is," Casement told her. "But don't fear, we'll get there. Just take it easy and sop up the sunshine. And if you look close enough and in the right places, there's a real scatter of interesting things to see along the way."

The sun climbed, and the air grew warmer, and the breath of sage, rendered out by the increasing heat, was a pungent flavor almost strong enough to taste. Sherry took off her coat and laid it across her lap. The road, though narrow enough in spots for the close-crowding brush to slap the buck-board wheels, was relatively smooth, and the steady clop-clop of the team's trotting hooves beat a relaxing rhythm.

To Sherry it seemed to be a land without a liv-ing thing in it anywhere until Casement began

56

pointing here and there with his whip. Where the sage thinned and gave back, Sherry saw long-eared desert jackrabbits crouched statue-still in dabs of scattered shade. And once, where the road topped a small rise allowing clear view of a flat to their right, Casement pointed again and spoke quickly. "Coyote!"

Sherry glimpsed the animal, saw the sharp, pricked ears, the pointed muzzle, the gaunt, furtive gray-brown shape. With a slinking twist of movement it was gone like a wisp of smoke.

"You've keen eyes," Sherry admitted. "If you hadn't pointed these things out I'd never have seen them."

Casement tipped a shoulder. "Just a matter of knowing where to look, and what for."

The miles slipped steadily backward, and imperceptibly the saddleback ridge grew closer while the edge of flat rimtop beyond became less misty suggestion and more solid reality.

Just as imperceptibly a feeling of complete ease and relaxation stole through Sherry Gault. Aside from the small sounds of their own movement, the jangle of the trace, the steady ruffle of jogging hooves, and the occasional grind of an iron-rimmed wheel over a rock outcrop hidden in the dust, this land was held by utter stillness. Here was isolation such as she had never before experienced. Never had she ridden free under a sky so vast and limitless or over a land that seemed to run on and on to some dim, misty infinity. In a strange, primal way it was frightening, and she said so in a small, half-whispering voice.

"When—when I try to contrast it with the world I've always known, it's like being transported back a thousand years or more. Everything is so big—big! You and I—we're just—well, nothing."

Casement grinned. "Specks of dust, that's all. If a spell of living in this country doesn't straighten out a person's thinking, then nothing ever will."

Abruptly they faced a dry wash that curved across the road. The buckboard pitched steeply down, jounced across a stretch of alkali-whitened gravel, then hauled up the far bank. Here, where the road leveled again, Casement pointed with his whip. "Yonder. Some Lazy L stuff. Generally is a few head of Larkin beef hanging around that little flat. It's one of Roy Larkin's salting grounds."

The cattle were burly, red-bodied animals with white faces. They stood with heads upthrown, watching the buckboard wheel past.

"That helped," Sherry announced with a small, uncertain laugh. "Seeing cattle, I mean. I needed something of the sort to prove I was still on the same old earth." She paused, thoughtful. "Larkin," she murmured. "Roy Larkin. Last night Kate—Miss Larkin—mentioned a brother . . . ?"

Casement nodded. "The same. You'll see their layout pretty soon."

Now the saddleback ridge was close at hand. The road looped past the end of it, and there in the middle distance, tucked in a pocket part way up the flank of the ridge, with a down-running line of green above and a wide smear of the same color beneath, was a cluster of ranch buildings.

"The Larkin place," said Casement. "Nights you can see their light from Clear Creek."

Out ahead it was no longer just the corner of a rim against the sky. Now it was a barrier filling miles of the horizon with a dark and frowning presence. The road, reaching onward, dipped and crossed another twisting dry-wash before climbing to a small crest whereon Casement drew rein and set his brake. He tossed a hand in an encompassing gesture.

"There it is. Clear Creek Ranch. And all yours!"

Sherry sat breathless, silent—completely stunned. She was looking across a valley that spread wide and long. Not a dry valley choked with sagebrush, but one that lay green with the curving line of a willow- and alder-banked watercourse threading the emerald meadows. The meadows were thickly dotted with cattle, fat cattle with red flanks and white faces that shone in the sun.

At the far edge of the valley and paralleling it, reared the rim, a massive black lava scarp, its sheer face broken here and there with talus slides and its crest furred with conifer. Crouched, so it

59

seemed, against the very base of the rim lay the ranch headquarters, the ranch house a gleam of white through the clean, green, tapered grace of spaced lombardy poplar trees.

Casement turned to the girl beside him. "Well, what do you think of it?"

Sherry gulped and stammered, "I—I don't know—what to think. I can't imagine—I mean I had no idea . . . I just—well . . . !" She lifted slim shoulders in a small, helpless way.

Casement smiled. "I told you it was quite a ranch."

Sherry gulped again and tried again. "You can't mean that—what we see out there—is mine?"

"All of it. Every acre, every head of stock. This rig we ride in and the team pulling it are yours. And there's more you can't see from here, like summer range up past the rim and another considerable chunk further south alongside of what Joe Moss owned. Yeah, you can put in a considerable stint of riding without getting off your own land."

Sherry went on stammering almost tearfully. "I—I just can't believe it. It simply can't . . . be real—not really real!"

"Just the same, it is," Casement assured her. "As real as the sun. Let's get along for a closer look."

The road led across the meadows to the creek. Cattle were on every hand. A newborn calf, licked dry and shining by its mother, stood braced on shaky, uncertain legs, staring with round, baby eyes out of a snowy-white face.

Casement chuckled. "That little bummer yonder, getting a first look at the world, is yours also. Wonder what it thinks of what it sees?"

"It's a darling thing!" Sherry cried in eagerness and excitement. "Oh, I tell you I simply can't believe it. Not all this—not—everything . . . !"

The road threaded the creek willows, sloping down to rippling, sun-dappled water that shimmered crystal-clear and sent up a moist, cool breath under the splashing hooves of the sorrels and the churning wheels of the buckboard. The horses tossed thirsty heads, and Casement, loosening the reins, let them stop and drink.

Sherry looked down at the clear, steady flow of the stream.

"So this is Clear Creek! After so much dry country, to see something like this . . . !"

"Good water and lots of it," stated Casement. "With it, in cattle country, you're a king. Without it, you're nothing. You should see where it comes from. Big Silver Spring. Right out of the lava. Winter, summer—it flows just the same. This valley may not be entirely a paradise, but in the eyes of a working cattleman it comes right close." He looked at Sherry and smiled as he spoke.

Beyond the creek the road climbed to a wide flat where stood the ranch headquarters, backed hard against the base of the rim. As they drew nearer, Sherry became increasingly aware of that brooding barrier of black lava. Even at a distance it had been impressive. Here, close up, its dark, frowning massiveness turned Sherry silent and wide of eye.

Casement sensed her thoughts. "At first it does overpower a little. Once you're used to it you see it as a good part of the world."

Also from a distance, headquarters had been just a gleam of white in the greenery of poplar trees, but now it showed itself to be an extensive spread. The ranch house itself, low and white, was at the forefront. Beyond, between it and the rim, were the various other ranch buildings—bunkhouse and cook shack, feed sheds and barns. On either hand was a sprawl of corrals, some holding cattle, some with horses in them.

A pair of riders were angling in across the meadows from the south, and in one of the smaller corrals two other punchers were shoeing saddle stock. A McNab shepherd dog came to meet the buckboard, and the sound of its welcoming bark brought still another ranch hand to the door of the cook shack, a leathery little man who moved with a limp and wore a flour sack tied at his waist as an apron.

"Gabe Tennant," Casement indicated, grinning. "Best all-around man I know. You name the job, and Gabe can do it, though the leg he broke a while back has slowed him up some. Looks like he's been busy preparing the feast of welcome. I'll call him and the other boys up and introduce them."

"Please!" Sherry exclaimed quickly. "Not—not just yet. I need more time to—to get adjusted to all this. I'm still not entirely sure it isn't all just a dream."

"Fair enough," Casement agreed. "Tell you what—you have a look at the ranch house while I put up the team."

He set the brake and jumped out. When Sherry hesitated at the high step he caught her by the elbows and lifted her lightly down, a move that left her flushed and slightly breathless. The strength of this lean brown man was steely.

A deep porch ran all across the front of the ranch house, and beside the door was a much-used easy chair, seated and backed with rawhide.

"Jack McCord's favorite spot in his later years," said Casement. "He'd sit there by the hour with his pipe, just looking—as he put it—at the prettiest picture in the world, at green pastures full of white-faced cattle. Come dusk, when a light would show over at the Larkin place, he'd say, 'Evenin', neighbor.' He was a great old man."

Casement opened the ranch house door. "Something else that's all yours. So make yourself at home."

He left her then, and Sherry moved slowly through the place, room by room. There were six rooms, two with stone hearths mellowed by the

63

smoke of many a fire built against winter's cold. The larger hearth was in the living room, which was spacious and lighted generously by several windows. The room holding the smaller fireplace was plainly a bedroom that now contained a bunk made up neatly with clean blue blankets.

The kitchen held a black iron cooking stove and an oilcloth-covered table. Another room with an outer as well as an inner door was evidently the ranch office. It contained an ancient rolltop desk piled with a miscellany of stock journals and several well-thumbed time and tally and account books of one sort or another. Here too were several round-backed chairs and a tall cupboard that filled one corner. A wall gun rack held several rifles, a shotgun, and a worn cartridge belt with a holstered six-shooter. There was a small heating stove whose chimney elbowed through the outer wall, then thrust upward past the eaves of the house. A great deal of living had been done in this particular room, and the old, cold odors of tobacco smoke were soaked into ceiling and walls beyond all removal.

Sherry was again finding need to revise a viewpoint. On the way to Battle Mountain by train she had, from her coach window, glimpsed occasional weather-faded buildings crouched gray and lonely in the far-running wilderness of sage, and these forlorn-appearing layouts had colored her previous opinion of a cattle ranch. Here, however, was something vastly different. Here was a roomy, stoutly built ranch house. And though the place had been strictly a bachelor layout, furnished with Spartan simplicity, it was evident that some proper feminine touches could brighten it up and make it a completely comfortable and livable home.

She went through it a second time, visualizing what could be done with it and trying to reach full understanding that all this was hers and hers alone. It was a staggering reality. Realization of ownership and what it could mean in all its possible ramifications was actually frightening and held her sober and subdued.

She returned to the front porch. The empty chair beside the door drew her interest. On impulse she dropped into it and let her glance rove over all that lay before her. With midday at hand the sun spread a shimmering haze across the miles, softening distant outlines, and under the brilliant pour of it—with a bit of fanciful license—the cattle in the meadows were not unlike red and white jewels strewn on emerald-green velvet. A small wind, slipping along the shadowed porch, carried a warm and fragrant breath.

Diffidence gripped her, a sense almost of helplessness. All this that was now hers—what was she going to do with it? What could she do with it? . . .

She left the porch. At the corrals the two riders who had come in across the meadows were talking with Luke Casement. One of them, agitated over something, swung an angry arm to emphasize his words.

Casement saw Sherry and joined her. His eyes were shadowed, and there was a hint of grimness about his lips.

"What did you think of the house? I told Gabe Tennant to clean things up."

"It is much more than I dreamed. I can hardly accept the reality of it," conceded Sherry soberly. She nodded toward the pair by the corral, now unsaddling their mounts. "Who are they?"

"Lee and Griff Toland. Two of ours. Come along and meet them."

The Toland brothers were typical sons of the saddle. Lean, supple men, brown of face and blue of eye. They touched their hats and murmured identical words.

"Happy to know you, ma'am."

Casement called the other two away from their horse-shoeing chore, giving their names as Sam Kell and Al Birch. Under the stains of sweat and dust they were the same type as the Tolands, lean and brown, with quick, direct glances. Sherry knew that silent opinions of her were being made and judgments rendered.

At the cook shack a triangle jangled insistently.

"Gabe's getting impatient," observed Casement. "We better answer."

The cook shack was strictly utilitarian. It held a long, plain wood table, with benches on either side and a round-backed chair at the head. In the rear of the room was the cook stove and other necessary kitchen equipment. The air swam with the fragrances of warm food.

Gabe Tennant stood beside the door, arms akimbo, eyes quick and terrier-bright under shaggy, grizzled brows.

"Someday," he threatened, "if you saddle-poundin' sons don't answer quicker to grub call, I'll lock the door and let you run hungry until next mealtime. I'd have done it today if it wasn't for the young lady. Even so, things could be near spoiled. You can't cook a little now and a little then and have it come out right."

Sherry smiled at the leathery old fellow. "I'm sure everything will be perfect. It smells gorgeous, and I'm ravenous."

Gabe's eyes sparkled. "Ma'am, you won't never leave this table hungry." He scuttled back to his stove, half-skipping to favor his damaged leg.

Casement held the chair at the end of the table for her, shaking his head when she would have demurred. "It's the boss's chair. Jack McCord always sat in it. Now it's your place."

Sherry's laugh was a trifle shaky. "I feel more like an intruder than anything else. And the more I see, the more I try and think, the more bewildered I am. Right now I haven't a single clear idea on my affairs—what they all are or what to do about them."

About to set a platter of steaks on the table, Gabe Tennant heard what she said and made a flat statement. "Don't you worry none, ma'am. Luke and the rest of us will take care of everything for you."

For the next few minutes the simple basic need of eating was all-important. Sherry thought of how nothing served better to acquaint humans and put them at their ease than breaking bread together. For the riders, reticent at first because of her presence, now began trading talk relating to various ranch affairs.

Sitting at Sherry's elbow, Casement broke in, "Where's Yance Hawn?"

"Headed out early this mornin'," Sam Kell informed him. "Said somethin' about prowlin' across the rim to see if that band of wild broncs were still runnin' the glades up there or if they'd gone back to the aspen swamps around Blue Lakes."

Griff Toland shook his head. "Horse crazy, Yance is. Still playin' with the idea of gettin' a rope on the big roan stallion leadin' that band."

Sam Kell grunted. "He ever does, he'll find he's roped himself to one wild waltz. That roan is at least a six-year-old, and after roamin' free that long it ain't about to take easy to the feel of saddle leather."

"Who," Sherry asked Casement, "is Yance Hawn?"

"Final member of our crew," Casement said tersely. "He could be doing something far more useful than burning out ranch saddle stock trying to rope a wild horse. I'll speak to him about that."

Al Birch, paying strict attention to his food, finished and got up to leave. At the door he stopped, stared, then made blunt announcement. "Company comin' in, Luke. Looks like Milo Hernaman and that shyster lawyer from town, Francis Quinnault."

Chapter FOUR

THE WARNING laid a moment of taut quiet across the room. Then Griff Toland gave harsh exclamation.

"After what he stirred up in town last night and what Lee and me met up with along the Running M range this morning, you'd figure Hernaman would go a little slow at showing up here. He must think he's God!"

Lee Toland, younger of the brothers and the most explosive, was quickly on his feet.

"I can sure change his mind on that point. Gabe, break out that old Winchester of yours!"

"Easy, easy!" soothed Casement. "All things in good time." He looked at Sherry. "It's you he'll want to talk to. And it might not be a bad idea if you listen. Or would you rather I send him on his way?"

69

Sherry understood what lay behind these words. A decision had to be made concerning the future of the Clear Creek Ranch. The sense of unreality and feeling of uncertainty she'd been battling surged anew. But she stood up and squared her slim shoulders.

"I'll hear what he has to say." She turned toward the door, then paused hesitantly. "I—I'd like you to be present, Mr. Casement."

"Of course." He went out the door with her.

A newly arrived buckboard had pulled to a halt under a poplar tree beside the ranch house, and Francis Quinnault was looping the halter rope of one of the team through an iron ring stapled to the tree trunk. Wearing a slouch hat and long gray linen duster, the lawyer—so Sherry thought—was as shabbily flamboyant as he'd appeared in the dining room of the Humboldt House last night.

A little apart and looking around possessively, Milo Hernaman stood, stocky and thickset. His boots were not those of a saddle man, being square of toe and low of heel, and he stood with feet spread and braced as though leaning into some invisible force and pushing it aside. Shadowed by a big white Stetson, his face was as blocky as the rest of him. His cheeks were florid, his jaw heavy and aggressive, with an almost brutal underthrust. His lips were wide and meaty and held a half-smoked cigar jutting at a combative angle. His nose was broad, thick, and flaring of nostril, and on either side of it, set far back under cotton-white

70

brows, his eyes were small and milk-pale and cold. They stared impassively as Sherry and Casement approached.

Not entirely sure of the situation, Francis Quinnault seemed about to speak, but Hernaman headed him off with a downward cut of his hand.

"I'll handle this, Quinnault." The pale, cold eyes fixed on Sherry. "I'm Milo Hernaman. I'm buying this ranch. I'll talk it over with you— alone."

The approach was startling, and it touched off an answering flare of resentment that turned Sherry's blue eyes stormy. She recalled the figure with the big white hat that had stood below her window in town last night and the pale blur of the face that had stared up at her. The quick revulsion she had felt then returned now, and she turned on a coldness of her own.

"If you speak with me at all, you will do so before Mr. Casement. He has my every confidence."

Hernaman repeated the dismissing, downward-cutting gesture with his hand. "Casement don't rate. He's just another two-bit cowhand. This is between you and me."

Sherry stood somewhat aghast. Here was a heavy, thrusting arrogance that was little short of preposterous. For the moment she was without words, but Casement took over for her.

"You heard the lady, Hernaman. If you've anything to say, you'll say it in front of me. Either that, or you can clear out. For you're in enemy territory and there are a couple of boys within call who'd like nothing better than a chance to drag you off the place at the end of a rope."

Hernaman shrugged and shifted his quick stare back to Sherry. "Where do we talk—here or inside?"

"The office will do." Again it was Casement. He nodded to Quinnault, who stood diffidently by. "You, too. Let's make this a discussion that everyone thoroughly understands."

Casement opened the office door and held the chair at the desk for Sherry. He folded his arms and leaned against the wall, watching Hernaman and Quinnault find chairs.

"All right," he drawled. "You can start in, Hernaman. So you're about to buy this ranch. What's your offer?"

Hernaman took his cigar from his lips and flicked the ash on the floor.

"Casement going to have all the sayso?" he demanded of Sherry.

She shook her head. "Not entirely. I'll speak for myself where I need to. But his question is a good one. How much do you offer, Mr. Hernaman?"

"Quinnault told you. Fifteen thousand."

"Ridiculous!" Sherry exclaimed. "You'll have to do better than that—much better."

She said it with emphasis, for now, quite suddenly, she was entirely sure of herself. All uncertainty, all hesitancy was gone. At this vital moment came clear realization of what her inheritance really meant to her. With it came full significance of ownership and full awareness of the responsibilities and obligations that accompanied that ownership. She repeated, with a curt decisiveness, "Yes, you'll have to do much better than that."

Hernaman lipped his cigar, then rolled it back and forth, squinting through the pale drift of its smoke. His glance wandered about the room, taking in each item that it held. It was as though he was measuring and calculating what he would do with the room, once it was his. He cleared his throat with an eruptive grunt.

"Fifteen thousand dollars is a lot of money. But I'm no piker. I'll make it twenty, which is more than the ranch is worth."

Sherry smiled in open derision. "We both know that isn't so. You're not even close, Mr. Hernaman."

The color in his florid cheeks deepened, and a glint of anger sharpened the paleness of his eyes. "It's as close as I'll get," he said roughly. "It will be that—or nothing."

"Well then, we'll leave it at nothing." Sherry's retort was swift. "Good day, Mr. Hernaman!"

He stood up, the glint in his eyes now a hard glitter. He took the cigar from his lips, holding it between folded fingers as he pointed it at her. "Maybe you don't savvy exactly what I mean, young lady. Either I buy this ranch for twenty thousand dollars, or I take it for nothing. Yes,

73

that's what I said—take it for nothing. Speaking straight out, I'd rather buy it than go after it the hard way. But if I have to go after it so, that's the way it will be. This ranch I want—and what I want real bad, I get!"

Sherry twisted in her chair and looked up at Casement. "Does he actually mean that?" There was a note of genuine wonder in her voice. "He'd actually—dare to . . . ?"

Casement nodded. "Remember what I told you last night at supper? Here is something else. There are already Dollar cattle on the Joe Moss range, which the Toland boys found out when they were down that way this morning. Also, some of Hernaman's hardcase saddle hands dusted up Griff and Lee with thirty-thirties when they rode a little bit too close. Oh, Mr. Hernaman moves fast— very fast—to get what he wants. And most of all he wants Clear Creek!"

Casement held her glance, and she knew that once again he was waiting for the all-important decision only she had the right to make. Matters had moved past the point of who she might sell to and for how much. Now the issue had become— was she or wasn't she going to sell at all?

An hour ago, faced with the same blunt issue, she would have been wallowing in indecision, but now she was ready with only one answer. She turned again to Hernaman, her head high. "Clear Creek ranch is not for sale, to you or anyone else.

74

Not at any price. I find that what my uncle, Jack McCord, left me means as much to me now as it did to him. So, for the last time—good day, Mr. Hernaman!"

Luke Casement's hand was a quick, strong touch on her shoulder. "Good girl! Hernaman, you got your answer. Now I've something to say. First, don't ever send anybody else after me like you sent Cass Dutcher. You do, I waste no time on them. But I'll look you up and make it a direct issue between you and me; I'll collect right out of your thieving hide. That's a promise you can pin on your wall, Hernaman—so you'll be sure to remember it!

"Secondly, don't try and move in on one inch of Clear Creek range. Jack McCord may be dead, but the men who would have backed his hand to any finish are still around and ready to do the same for his niece, Miss Gault. Finally, get your damn cows off the Joe Moss range. You may have got rid of the poor devil who owned that range, but you don't move in on it this easy, Hernaman. There's a limit to what decent men will stand from you. I guess that about covers everything, so now you can do what the lady suggests. Get out!"

Milo Hernaman moved to the door, paused, and partially turned. Color still burned high in his cheeks, and the glitter in his pale, cold eyes hung on. "You, young lady," he told Sherry harshly, "are a giddy little fool, with no idea of what you're letting yourself in for. And you"—here his glance settled on Casement, and his tone turned sinister —"you won't live to see the end of summer!"

He went out then, his steps a hard stamping. Francis Quinnault, edgy and nervous, also paused at the door as though to speak. Casement discouraged him curtly. "Don't bother, Quinnault. Anything you say won't count, now. But I've a suggestion you can ponder on—you and Broady Ives. Be sure you don't make the mistake of backing the wrong horse. If you do, there won't be much future for you in these parts. You can tell Broady that for me when you get back to town."

Casement listened to the buckboard rattle away, after which he came around to face a sober, troubled Sherry Gault.

"Am I?" she asked.

"Are you—what?"

"What he said. A giddy little fool. Because perhaps he's right. It was easy enough to say what I did—that I wouldn't sell, not ever. But now, when I think of the things he threatened . . . ! Could he have really meant—all of it?"

"At the moment, probably. But when he stops to consider matters a little more calmly, he could change his mind. A lot could depend on how we handle ourselves here at Clear Creek."

"How do you mean?"

Casement hauled up a chair, straddled it, and folded his arms across the back of it. "Like this. For his last several years, Jack McCord was in no

76

shape to mix in any kind of an actual physical fight himself; yet during that time Milo Hernaman wanted the ranch just as badly as he does now. Just the same, he shied away from a showdown for possession. Aside from Jack McCord, here at Clear Creek we're just as strong now as we were then. The only difference is the authority old Jack represented. Now the authority is yours, which is the angle Hernaman is gambling on."

Sherry considered gravely. "How . . . gambling? Jack McCord represented lawful ownership then. Now I do. Where is the difference as Milo Hernaman sees it?"

"The will to resist. Before Jack McCord would have let Hernaman take one little inch of range away from him—or from a neighbor like Joe Moss—he'd have fought to his last dime, his last drop of blood. Which Hernaman damn well knew, and it shaped up as a situation he didn't care to tackle."

"But now," Sherry said, "he feels I won't have the courage to fight back, is that it?"

Casement's glance became very steady and his words quiet. "That's it. And will you? Will you back the men who are ready and willing to fight for you and your ranch? Will you stand behind them in every way no matter what it costs, in money or blood?"

Sherry's eyes grew big as she assessed the prospect. "I—I don't know," she answered honestly. "I—I hope I would. Oh, I've no fear for myself.

But to have others hurt—made to suffer because of me—I just don't know!"

"It's a fact that has to be faced," Casement warned tersely. "Once it is—once things start—there can be no weakening, no retreat."

Sherry struck her hands together in a gesture of worriment.

"It's horrible even to think about," she cried softly. "You heard what he said to you—that you'd be dead before the end of summer."

"I heard," Casement admitted wryly. "He was just getting rid of an overdose of spleen. No doubt it's what he'd like to see, but I'll have something to say about the matter."

Sherry stared at him, her blue eyes wide. "Luke Casement, I'm—I'm scared!"

He grinned. "You wouldn't be normal if you weren't. In his time, one way or another, Milo Hernaman has scared a lot of people. But he couldn't scare Jack McCord—or lick him. And he can't lick us now if we show him the same face old Jack did."

Again Sherry considered soberly. "If Uncle Jack were alive today, what would his first move be?"

"He'd run those Dollar cattle off the Joe Moss range."

"And if Hernaman tried to stop him . . . ?"

Casement shrugged. "He'd run 'em off anyhow."

"But you said the Toland brothers were shot at this morning by some of Hernaman's men. Wouldn't they shoot again?"

"Probably. Only this time we'd shoot back. Which makes a difference. Griff and Lee Toland weren't armed this morning. But from now on every Clear Creek rider will carry a gun. And use it, if necessary."

Sherry framed her face in her hands, pressing her cheeks to whiteness. "To think that in this day and age, such things are possible . . . !" she half-whispered, as though to herself alone.

"It's big country out here," reminded Casement. "Big country—and new country in comparison to where you came from. We have a surface of written law, of course, but if for some reason it fails to reach deep enough to touch real justice, then the old rules and ways take over."

"But I've no right to expect you—or others—to risk so much for me or my affairs. Oh, Luke—I never dreamed I'd have to face up to anything like this—not ever."

She used his name with a disarming natural-ness, and he thought again how appealingly young and uncertain she was. He reassured her gently, "Don't worry about me or the rest of the crew. We're part of this ranch, and it's part of us. That is how any worthwhile puncher feels toward the outfit he rides for. And he'll fight for his hire. Over the years, Jack McCord may have made a hiring

79

mistake or two, but for the most part he signed on only top hands. So long as you stand behind them, they won't let you down."

Echoing in through the afternoon warmth came the beat of approaching hoofs. Casement stepped to the door and looked out. Watching him, Sherry saw a smile of welcome crinkle his eye corners. Then, as the hoofbeats eased to a stop, they heard Kate Larkin's voice.

"If you're wondering why I'm here, my friend, it's to see if that waif from the East, Sherry Gault, is being properly treated. I saw her with you when you drove past our place, and I saw Milo Hernaman and Francis Quinnault come this way too, a while ago. And just now I passed them on the road, heading back to town. Luke, what did you do to Hernaman? He looked mean enough to sweat rattlesnake venom."

She came into the office, breezy, vigorous, moving with carefree, long-legged grace. She smiled at Sherry.

"Greetings, neighbor! Now you've seen your Clear Creek Ranch, what do you think of it?"

"I'm still trying to get used to it," Sherry told her, warming to this direct and friendly girl. "It is much more than I dreamed!"

"Hah! Let's hope it grows on you then until you decide to keep it."

"That's already been decided. I am keeping it."

"Wonderful!" Kate Larkin exclaimed. "That explains thoroughly why Milo Hernaman was aching so on his way back to town. He couldn't buy you out at his own thieving price, and he couldn't scare you out—is that it?"

"He scared me," Sherry admitted. "And I still am."

"But not enough to keep her from turning him down flat," put in Casement. "Now, while you two talk things over, I'll go give the boys the word —that Clear Creek is still a going ranch. They've been anxious to know, one way or the other."

He went out. Kate Larkin looked at Sherry.

"So Mr. Hernaman was full of threats, was he?"

Sherry nodded. "He said if I didn't accept the price he offered, he'd take over anyway and I'd get nothing. He also threatened Luke—Mr. Casement —telling him he'd be dead before the end of summer."

"That bullying, greedy pirate!" exploded Kate Larkin angrily. "He would talk that way."

"And I don't see how he can even dare threaten, let alone actually do such things," Sherry said, shaking her head. "As though there were no such thing as law; as though other people had no rights at all."

"Money, my dear—money! That and politics. Milo Hernaman owns a string of ranches all across the state. Big ranches, rich ones. He's long wanted to add Clear Creek to the string, figuring it would give him power in this county, as his other holdings have done in other counties. He might even have ideas of putting together enough

81

political and financial weight to run the state. I wouldn't put it past him, for he's power crazy. Just the same, he didn't dare try any of his tricks here while Jack McCord was alive."

"But now he does," said Sherry soberly. "Seeing me as just a poor, weak woman, no doubt."

"You're not weak," Kate Larkin declared emphatically. "Not as long as you have Luke Casement on your side. Great as he was at one time, toward the last Jack McCord was just a sick, tired old man who could never have stood up to Milo Hernaman if he hadn't had Luke to lean on."

Sherry stood up and moved restlessly about. "I said I was scared, and I am. Not for myself, of course. But I don't want to think of people being hurt or—or worse, because of me and my affairs." She paused, her eyes going big and dark at the thought. She shook her head. "No, I can't bear to think of that."

"Then don't," said Kate briskly. "It may never happen. At least we'll hope it won't. And remember this—the trade of a saddle man is not the safest in the world. Every day your riders go at their routine jobs they face hazards of some sort. Why only last year my brother and I lost one of our best men. He was chasing strays out of some rough malpais. His horse fell and threw him head-first into a ledge of lava. Rowdy Simms was one of my favorites, and I wept for a week. But life goes on, and we all have to move with it. My father used to say that anyone who was afraid to face up to the

82

costs of life didn't deserve any of its rewards." She put an arm about Sherry.

"How about looking at the pleasanter things," she went on, "such as how to dress up this house a little, now you're about to start living in it?"

Sherry stiffened, dismayed. "My personal things! They're all in town. I can't stay here tonight without them."

"Anything you need for the night, I'll loan you," promised Kate. "Now about this house, which I know is as bare as a monk's cell. Men, bless 'em, if left to themselves, seem content to live in a bare wood box. I've always itched for the chance to do something here, and I used to tell Jack McCord that and scold him about it. But he'd just boom his great laugh at me, the lovable old devil."

It took a little effort for Sherry to shake the mood Milo Hernaman and his threats had left her with, but Kate's enthusiasm and drive were catching, and a large part of the afternoon slipped away while they planned and plotted. They ended up standing on the porch of the house, where the westering sun's slanting rays came in on them.

"You've been very kind," Sherry told her companion. "You've made my—well, decision to stay here more comforting."

"And you, my dear," Kate returned, "are a god-send to me. To have someone of my own kind and age handy to visit with means more than you'll ever dream. Men are just fine and dandy, but when you see nothing but the dratted critters day

83

in and day out—well, a gal can get kind of scratchy. Oh-oh! Here's one of the brutes now."

Luke Casement was heading over from the bunkhouse. "Have a good visit?" he asked.

"The best," Kate told him. "Go saddle yourself a horse, cowboy. You're riding home with me to bring back some things this new and valued neighbor of mine needs to make her comfortable for the night. Why on earth didn't you insist she bring her luggage out from town?"

Casement showed a small grin. "Didn't want to risk an argument. Afraid she'd spook on me and not ride out at all." He looked at Sherry. "I could send one of the boys after your things, though it would be late by the time he got back. Mrs. Megarry could get them together."

Sherry shook her head. "That isn't necessary. Kate is loaning me all I'll need for tonight; and tomorrow, first thing, she and I are driving to town to get a number of things besides my luggage. We're going to dress this house up a little."

"Well, I can understand why you'd want to. Jack McCord never went in for more than the stark necessities. Not that he was in any way a miser, understand. He always said he just didn't want to be bothered."

He went to catch and saddle, and presently he and Kate rode off together, jogging side by side. Kate was saying something to him in her quick, eager way, and Casement, half-turned in his saddle to listen, was smiling at her.

84

Watching them, it came to Sherry that some sort of rapport existed between this breezily direct ranch girl and the lean, brown, cool-eyed man in whose hands now rested the future of Clear Creek Ranch. It was, Sherry decided, something deeper than mere friendship, recalling Kate Larkin's open terror when Luke Casement had faced Cass Dutcher's deadly venom on Battle Mountain's street, and Kate's tears of relief and flaming pride as she exulted over the manner in which Casement handled the gunman.

Once more in Jack McCord's favorite chair by the ranch house door, Sherry settled down to watch the afternoon run out. As the sun lowered, shadows took shape at the edge of the willows along the creek, small and hesitant at first, but growing bolder and more widespread with each passing minute.

Some of the day's warmth leaked away, and colder air moved along the porch. Down in the meadows cattle began bunching up, with stragglers lining in from here and there. Well distant to the north, Sherry's roving glance picked up another flicker of movement that became a thin file of antelope stealing warily in from the great sprawl of sage beyond the valley's far rim. The animals vanished in the creek willows and, minutes later, having had the drink they came for, reappeared and drifted back again into the loneliness of distance.

Up from the creek coverts carried the clear,

sweet sundown call of quail, which hinted of wistful loneliness, and in the poplar trees beyond the porch the chatter of sparrows grew subdued, almost sleepy.

It was, thought Sherry, a kind of world that she, only a few weeks ago, had had little idea existed. But here it was now, spread out all about her—with so much of it that was hers and hers alone if she could hold it. And would she, she wondered, ever fully catch up with the reality of that fact? . . .

Spur chains jangled at the end of the porch. A rider stood there, hat in hand. He was narrow of hip and wide of shoulder. His hair was sleek and black, his cheeks slightly swarthy, and his teeth shone white as he smiled and spoke.

"I'm Hawn, ma'am—Yance Hawn. Just got in off the rim. The boys told me our new boss was on hand, so I figured I'd best come over and announce myself."

He moved along the porch and stood before her. His eyes were black and full of a hot pride, and he was, thought Sherry, about as handsome a man as she had ever seen. She covered a surge of startled feeling with a hesitant laugh.

"I'm not much of a boss, I'm afraid. You'll take your orders from Luke— Mr. Casement. He knows what it is all about, while I know very little about a ranch. Did you get your wild horse?"

His eyes narrowed slightly. "How'd you know I was after one?"

"I heard the other riders say you were. Did you catch it?"

"No, ma'am—I didn't. But I saw it. And ma'am—there is some animal! I'd give a pretty to put a rope on that chunk of horseflesh."

"Why that, when there is a corral full of them you can ride?"

He brought out tobacco and papers and deftly rolled a cigarette. When he spoke it was past his cupped hands as he nursed a sputtering sulphur match to full flame and touched it to his cigarette. Also, past those cupped hands, his glance was disturbingly intent. "Think of the fun it would be, breaking a bronc or any other wild critter to rein."

Sherry stood up and turned to the door. "I'd prefer to think of it as still running wild and free, and I suggest we leave it that way."

"Yes, ma'am," drawled Yance Hawn. "If that's how you want it, I reckon that's how it will be."

He went off, spur rowels spinning and clashing, his white teeth glinting in another smile.

There, decided Sherry soberly, *goes one who thinks very well of himself. Rather too well!* . . .

Chapter FIVE

IT WAS FULL dark when Luke Casement returned from the Larkin ranch. Sherry had a lamp going in the office, and even as Casement delivered a small gripsack to her, Gabe Tennant beat up the supper call on his cook-shack triangle.

Sherry looked toward the sound. "Apparently Uncle Jack didn't use the kitchen of this ranch house very much. The shelves are practically empty. Would it be all right if I ate with the crew again tonight?"

"All right? Of course," said Casement quickly. "Any time or all the time. This is your ranch, your food, your crew, remember? If you haven't the right to eat when and where they do, I wouldn't know who has."

"I don't want the men to resent me or feel uncomfortable with me around. I don't want to inflict myself on them."

"Good Lord, girl—why should they resent you? Actually, they'll be looking forward more than ever to mealtimes with you present. Or didn't you realize that you are something extra special around here?"

Sherry flushed, her laugh small and uncertain.

"I don't feel extra special. Like I told you before, my real feeling is that of an outsider, a foreign intruder who is reluctantly accepted but not warmly welcome."

"Then it's a feeling to get rid of. You're a highly attractive young woman newly arrived at a ranch that hasn't seen much of your kind in the past—which makes you more than welcome." Casement paused, chuckling. "Speaking of that empty kitchen you found, about the only cooking ever done in it were the few times Kate Larkin put together a meal for Jack McCord on special occasions. I asked him one time why he ever bothered to build a kitchen in the house in the first place. He had to scratch his head over that before saying it was because no house was complete unless there was a kitchen in it, even if it was never used."

"Well," declared Sherry, "starting tomorrow evening when I get back from town, I'll see that it gets all the use it has missed in the past."

Casement went away to put up his horse. Standing in front of the small square mirror on the wall of the room that held the freshly blanketed bunk, Sherry brushed up with some of the feminine gear Kate Larkin had sent. Finished, she inspected her reflection with a critical eye.

Highly attractive. That was what Luke Casement had said. Silently and honestly she admitted there was some truth to the statement, and she supposed it was quite legitimate to find satisfaction in it. . . .

She went back to the office, left the lamp there turned low, then stepped out into the night. Almost instantly the staggering physical impact of the rim struck her. Sheer and black, it lifted against the first scatter of early stars with a presence almost awesome. Looking up at it, Sherry caught her breath.

Beyond the interval the light at the cook-shack windows and open door beckoned, and she headed toward that warm cheer. But within a few yards she stopped short, brought up by words carrying through the dark from over by the corrals, words by Luke Casement, curt with authority.

"You're hired to look after ranch affairs, Hawn —not spend your time roving around up back of the rim trying to locate and run down some wild bronc. If you've any idea that because Jack Mc-Cord isn't around any more to keep an eye on things we're about to slack off on regular ranch chores, you're way wrong. From now on, remember that!"

The answer came in Yance Hawn's drawl, though now a drawl that was hard and sharp, holding none of the lazy ease Sherry had heard in it before.

"How'd I know what was going on? You were holed up in town, and nobody gave out morning orders for the day, like usual. So I took a run up past the rim, which wasn't breaking no law. If you'd have been on the job, instead of taking it easy in town, I'd have been on the job too. So quit

90

throwing the rawhide at me. Because I just won't take it!"

"The other boys didn't need to be told to know there was work to be done. And when you need the rawhide, you'll take it or take your time," Casement stated flatly. "I'm still riding boss of this ranch, and until Sherry Gault says different, I stay riding boss!"

"Maybe one of these fine days, Sherry Gault will say different," retorted Hawn. "And then we'll see—we'll see . . . !" The taunting words ran off into silence.

Disturbed, and with some of the newly found edge of anticipation taken off the evening, Sherry went on to the cook shack. Gabe Tennant had a wide smile of welcome for her. He limped quickly around to the head of the table and pulled out her chair for her. She thanked him but protested at the same time.

"You mustn't bother so with me, Gabe. I expect no special favors or treatment. I'm just part of the ranch now, like everyone else."

Gabe shook a stubborn head. "No, ma'am—you're way more than that. You're a lady, and I'm goin' to see you're treated like one any time and all the time. Anybody who figgers different can expect a real quarrel with me. Yes, sir—a real quarrel!"

The men came in—Sam Kell, Al Birch, and the Toland brothers. They flashed quick glances and furtive nods at her, then took their places and

91

paid strict attention to the food in front of them. Sherry smiled to herself. They were, she thought amusedly, almost like small boys. . . .

Not so, however, with Yance Hawn. He came in with the hot fires of a latent anger burning in his black eyes as he looked around. Then he smiled and came over to sit at Sherry's elbow in the place Luke Casement had occupied at the midday meal.

"Now this," he drawled, "is a sure-enough pleasure I hadn't figured on. Not the chance to eat with a lady."

An invisible but definite ripple of feeling ran around the table. Gabe Tennant limped over from his stove, his glance sharp, his words soft. "Wouldn't be makin' a mistake of any kind, would you, Hawn?"

Yance Hawn looked up at him, black eyes suddenly as hard as glass. "Not me, old man. But you are, trying to tell me my business. Get back to your cooking!"

From the doorway, Luke Casement spoke evenly. "It's all right, Gabe. Let's everybody enjoy their supper."

He took a place further down the table beside Sam Kell and began discussing ranch problems, his voice low and quiet.

It was not the most comfortable meal Sherry had ever sat down to, for despite Casement's soothing words the room filled with a palpable tension, and it was plain whose manner had caused it. So when Yance Hawn made several attempts to strike up a conversation with her, Sherry discouraged him with monosyllabic answers, until he presently lapsed into a sulky silence, finished his meal quickly, and went out.

Later, when Sherry was ready to leave, Casement came over to her. "If you're not too tired to listen, there are some more business angles we should go over. In the office?"

Sherry nodded. "Of course."

Outside, she paused for another look at the rim. The stars were out now in all their fullness, flinging their bright, cold glitter all across the great dark arch of the night sky. Some almost seemed to perch on the rim's crest. Sherry hugged herself. "It's grim, vast—wild," she murmured. "I wonder if I'll ever get used to it?"

"Of course you will," comforted Casement. "You'll come to miss it, too, when you're away from it. Because, even if we won't admit it, all of us crave some kind of assurance and proof that our world is stable and permanent. And that tough old black lava rim has been there since all the yesterdays and will still be there through all the tomorrows. So, once you're used to it, it's a comfort."

He was a tall, lean, shadowy figure beside her. In the darkness she could not make out his expression, but his words had startled her, and she spoke wonderingly. "Luke Casement, you surprise me."

He laughed lightly. "Didn't mean to start expounding. Still and all, when a man does a lot of riding alone, he gets to thinking about such things. And sometimes he comes up with a fair answer."

In the office he turned up the lamp to full glow. He brought out a battered metal box from the tall corner cupboard, put it on the desk, and opened it. Sherry found herself looking at a rather considerable amount of money in bills and a canvas sack that was heavy and bulging with coins.

"Around eight hundred to a thousand," Casement judged. "Ready cash to pay the crew and also house money, as Jack McCord used to call it. And when you're in town tomorrow, drop in to the bank and have a talk with Dan Vincent. He's a good man, Dan is, and an old friend of Jack McCord. He'll advise you right on money matters and tell you how much your bank balance is."

"You mean," Sherry said, caught up again with wonder, "that along with all the rest—there's also money in the bank?"

"Sure." Casement nodded. "At least ten thousand or thereabouts. Old Jack never went for storing up more than that. He liked to turn it back into the ranch, buying up more range and bringing in blooded breeding stock to grade up the herd."

Sherry laughed shakily, swinging her head from side to side. "I never—I just never—never . . . ! Luke Casement, almost at any minute I'm liable to break down and weep on your shoulder."

He chuckled. "Go ahead, if it'll make you feel

better. Glad I was able to head you away from Francis Quinnault and talk you into coming out to look things over?"

"I'll never get over being thankful!" she exclaimed fervently. "I'm beginning to realize how much I owe you."

"You don't owe me a thing. I just work for you."

He closed the money box and put it back in the cupboard. He brought something else to lay on the desk before her. Now she did stare. For she was looking at a blue-black slim-barreled revolver.

"Ever shoot one of these?" Casement asked.

Sherry shook her head violently. "Never—and I don't want to."

"Then, among other things, I'll have to teach you how."

"For heaven's sake—why?"

He pulled up a chair, got out his pipe, packed and lit it, then spoke past a mouthful of smoke. "Have you any kin left in the east?"

"No—none. I lost my mother three years ago this month. Since then I've been entirely alone."

"Then you've no reason ever to return to the East?"

"None whatever, except perhaps on a casual visit to renew a few old friendships."

Casement nodded. "Fair enough. Let's look at the future. You now own a ranch, the biggest and best around here, which makes you a person of considerable importance. But you know nothing

95

about that ranch. Yet you can't afford to leave the responsibility of running it up to any hired hand. You'll get a lot of help from the hired hands, of course, but when the blue chips are really down, there has to be a boss. The boss, like it or not, is you. And that means you'll have to make certain necessary decisions from time to time that are bound to crop up. And that in turn means there is a lot for you to learn about land and cattle —and human nature.

"You won't be spending all your time here at headquarters. You'll be out checking up on range and stock and all manner of other ranch affairs. And you won't always have someone else with you. A lot of the time you'll be riding alone. Now we know what Milo Hernaman has threatened. While it could be mostly bluff, we wouldn't be smart if we didn't believe him and prepare accordingly. I'm sure you understand what all that could mean."

He paused and ran a match across the bowl of his pipe. Then he looked at her with a direct gravity. "I've said that you were highly attractive. I'll say it again, because you are. And though most of the people around here—as is true of other parts of the country—are the pure quill, there are some of the other sort. And should a very pretty young woman happen to meet with one of such while alone, to have a gun like this loaded and handy and within reach could be a very comforting thing. For instance Kate Larkin, about as able and self-sufficient a member of her sex as I know of, always has a gun of some sort with her when she rides or drives alone. She knows how to use it too. So . . ." He shrugged expressively.

Sherry stared at the revolver. "It looks—very deadly."

"When pointed right, it is." Casement lifted the weapon, swung out the empty cylinder, and spun it across the palm of his hand. "Harmless now because it's empty. But one of these days before long we'll give it a workout and get acquainted with it. Now, something else. Ever been on a horse?"

"Some. There was a riding academy near where I lived. I spent some time along the bridle paths with an instructor. But I brought no riding clothes with me."

"Something you can take care of in town tomorrow. The ranch has a running account with Horton and Giles, the big general store. They handle everything. So stock up on what you want. Kate Larkin will advise you if you need help." He blew tobacco smoke toward the ceiling and peered through it thoughtfully before nodding. "I guess that about takes care of everything for now. Would you have anything special to get off your mind, boss?" He grinned at her.

"Yes." Her chin lifted. "Don't call me boss. I certainly don't feel like one. To you I'm Sherry, and to me you're Luke. For us to continue being formal in any way would be silly. Agreed?"

His grin became a chuckle. "Agreed. You're learning—and fast. Anything more?"

She nibbled a red underlip in momentary indecision. Then she nodded. "On my way to supper I overheard what passed between you and Yance Hawn over by the corrals. And at the supper table I got the feeling he wasn't too popular with the other men. If that is so, what's the reason?"

"Yance," observed Casement carefully, "is his own worst enemy. He can be a top hand when he wants to. Trouble is—he doesn't always want to be. Maybe Jack McCord spoiled him some, as he was one of Jack's favorites. He's a little like a bronc that was never thoroughly broken—you have to keep a tight rein on him."

Casement stood up and moved to the door. "You've had a long day of it. And if I know Kate Larkin, she'll be over here after you before sunup tomorrow. So you best get some rest. Good night."

The blanketed bunk was warm and comfortable. Luke Casement had certainly spoken the truth about it's having been a long day—a long and almost unbelievable day! Never, Sherry mused drowsily, could anyone's life have taken a more abrupt right-angle turn than had her own. Certainly no one of her age and meager experience ever had to make so many important and irrevocable decisions in so short a time. The marvel of it was that she'd been able to do this with such a feeling of definite certainty.

Arriving at Battle Mountain just twenty-four hours ago, she had been shaken and uncertain about many things. But today, faced with all the facts and the necessity of saying yes or no clearly and with certain purpose, she had not wavered. It was, she thought, as if some unguessed and unforeseen destiny had taken over and manipulated matters. Or had it been the solid presence and deftly guiding hand of a lean, brown, steely man named Luke Casement? . . .

Well, whatever the reason, what she ever had been was all behind her now—and whatever the future held, she was eager to meet it.

She snuggled deeper into her blankets and fell asleep thinking of that big black rim out there standing guard under the stars. . . .

A stir of activity in the kitchen and the wafted fragrance of morning coffee awakened her. Only the thinnest hint of daylight showed at her window, and the air was cold and knife-keen. Wondering at the presence in the kitchen, she pushed up on one elbow and lifted a cautious call, hoping she was right.

"Kate! Would that be you? Not this early, for goodness' sake!"

"Day is beginning to peek in over the rim," Kate Larkin returned cheerfully. "It's time to be up and doing."

Never had Sherry dressed more swiftly, fumbling a bit in the cold, gray gloom of the false dawn. Alternately hugging herself and rubbing her chilled cheeks, she hurried into the kitchen, where lamp glow spread welcoming cheer across the room.

She put an arm about Kate Larkin and gave her a squeeze. "You wonder! How do you do it? Luke Casement warned me you'd be over early. I'm sorry I wasn't up and ready. But to me it seems like the middle of the night."

Kate laughed. "Another custom of the country for you to get used to. We don't like to waste any daylight, early or late."

The stove was creaking with heat, and Sherry hovered over it. A coffeepot steamed, and bacon was sputtering in a pan. Kate opened the oven door, holding the lamp high for a peek at a pan of browning biscuits.

Sherry indicated the preparing food. "Where did you find these ingredients? I looked for some last night, but there was nothing on these shelves. So I ate supper with the men."

Kate laughed again in her easy, merry way. "I raided Gabe Tennant's pantry in the cook shack. He was just beginning to stir around and was still in his underwear. He looked like nothing so much as a grizzled, molting, scandalized old owl. And he was cranky as sin. Here's a bit of advice for you, my dear. Eat with the crew at noon or at night if you want. But never—never, for heaven's

100

sake—eat breakfast with them. Because early morning is the ornery hour for most male critters. That's when they grump and growl around until you feel like wringing their necks. So in town we still stock up with all you need to fill your own kitchen shelves, and you'll be able to do your breakfasting right here as mistress of your own domain. And after that see that you make it a privilege for any of your crew to ever eat with you. Now let's sit down and dig in. We've a full day ahead."

True dawn was at hand by the time they were ready to leave. Kate had tied her team to the iron ring in the poplar tree, and Luke Casement was there beside it when they went out. While untying the team for them he asked Kate, amusement in his tone, "What the devil did you do to Gabe Tennant? I just came from the cook shack, and he was slamming pots and pans around while mentioning your name and mumbling something about a shameless hussy who invaded a man's privacy in the middle of the night."

Between gusts of choked laughter, Kate explained. "And oh, Luke," she finished, wiping her eyes, "he was the funniest-looking old fellow, all touseled and blinking and bewildered. As I told Sherry here, he made me think of a startled owl."

Turning the eager team loose, Casement let go his own shout of laughter.

Kate drove with expert touch. The buckboard whisked down the slight slope and out on to the flat of the meadows, past cattle that were beginning to scatter and graze. Sherry twisted and looked back. Beyond the towering black face of the rim the sky was a pearl-gray stained with rose, but the gulf of deep, deep shadow at the rim's base was still held in a veil of swimming night mists.

She straightened around, her eyes narrowed against the chill rush of air. So from now on, this was to be her world, one anchored by a great, frowning scarp of black lava. Her new world was still primitive, still savage to some degree, for it held people who could, on occasion, still fight and die on the streets of its towns. Yet for the most part, these same people owned a great kindness and could laugh with the heartiest of humor. In them there was none of the hypocrisy Sherry had met up with so much in the other and supposedly more civilized company she had known in the East.

The buckboard wheels churned through the creek crossing and straightened out on the longer run across the valley flats beyond. A small warmth touched the nape of Sherry's neck, and abruptly there was a long, dancing shadow running out ahead of the team. The sun was taking a first look at the new day.

They topped the valley rim, and as Luke Casement had on the ride in yesterday, Kate indicated the Lazy L headquarters with a wave of her whip.

"Home to me," she said. "I'll expect a visit

from you as soon as you get organized. After that, I want to see you riding this way often."

They wheeled on into the long slopes of sagebrush and presently passed the Lazy L salting ground and the steep-walled dry wash beyond. Some mile or two further along, Kate pulled the brake abruptly and hauled her team to a stop. Balancing lithely, she stood up for a better look at something she had spied off to the right of the road. She stared for a moment before dropping back to the seat. "Hold on to everything," she advised tersely. "Some rough going ahead."

She reined her team through a narrow break in the wall of sagebrush and on across a considerable expanse of dry lake, dodging some, but not all, of the scatter of lava chunks and lesser clumps of sage that dotted the area. The buckboard lurched and twisted over those which could not be dodged, until Sherry thought it would come apart.

But it did not, and at the far edge of the dry lake Kate pulled to a stop near a white-faced steer that stood on three legs with back humped and head sagging. Its fourth leg swung limp and twisted below the knee joint. The hapless animal made no move, paid no attention to their approach. Its eyes were half-closed, its body gaunt and ribby. Against the ribs a brand stood out that looked to Sherry like the letter L lying on its side.

"One of ours," explained Kate. "When I saw it I wondered what it was doing way out here alone. Now I know. By some mischance it's collected a

103

broken leg. The poor brute can't get to either water or food and is dying by inches. So—there is only one thing to do." She set the brake and handed the reins to Sherry. "This team has heard a gun before now, but if they should turn squirmy and try to run, haul back on the reins and head them into the heaviest sage. That'll stop them."

Before Sherry could reply or protest, Kate was out of the rig. From a worn, heavy leather scabbard slung low behind the seat, she drew a Winchester carbine. She swung the lever of the gun, lifting a cartridge from magazine to chamber. She moved to within a couple of yards of the crippled steer, lifted the carbine, and aimed carefully. When the gun flung out its hard, flat report, the steer collapsed instantly.

The team made one startled lunge, then quieted as Sherry pulled back on the reins, a little breathless and not entirely sure of herself. For a time Kate Larkin looked down at the luckless animal at her feet; then she came quietly back to the buckboard. She slid the carbine into its scabbard, climbed in, and took over the reins.

"A shame and a waste of what was once a first-grade beef critter," Kate said. "But there was no chance to save it, so the humane thing to do was put it out of its misery." She kicked off the brake and swung the rig back across the dry lake and into the town road once more.

Quiet up to now, Sherry spoke. "Again and again I am amazed by this country and the people in it. Just now—what you did—why I'd never be able to do that—not ever. I wouldn't have the nerve."

"Oh yes you would—and will someday. Besides, it wasn't a question of having nerve. Just human compassion for a poor, dumb, suffering animal that was doomed anyway. Better it die swiftly in one crashing instant than to go down slowly from hunger and thirst with the scavengers waiting to pounce. See, the buzzards are gathering already." She indicated several circling black dots dropping swiftly out of the sky.

Sherry grimaced. "There's a lot of cruelty in the world, isn't there?"

"And a lot of beauty, too," fenced Kate. "So don't let this spoil your day."

Under the sun's growing force it became a warming world. They drove on in silence for a time, with Sherry content to leave it so until something else at the back of her mind began to stir.

"I suppose," she ventured, "you know a rider of mine named Yance Hawn?"

"I know him."

"What is your opinion of him?"

"Yance Hawn," said Kate flatly, "is one of the two big mistakes Jack McCord ever made in human nature. The other was in putting any of his affairs in the hands of such as Francis Quinnault. Yance's father and Jack McCord were old friends. Dying, Yance's father asked old Jack to keep a protective eye on the son. Which Jack did in the best way he could, hiring him on and giving him every chance to make something of himself. Had he done so, Yance might have shared in Jack McCord's will. But Yance was and is and will always be a cheap, sly, full-time stinker, much too fond of his own good looks. He is out to make a fool of every gullible female he meets up with. And from all reports," ended Kate with a dry, biting sarcasm, "he's enjoyed considerable success at it. To repeat, I see him as a conceited, no-good stinker!" She looked at Sherry with a narrow directness. "What made you ask?"

"I wondered, that's all," explained Sherry simply. "Because, while eating with the crew last night, I got the impression he wasn't exactly popular with the rest of the men. I asked Luke Casement about it. He admitted Yance was spoiled and a little hard to handle, but he did not add much beyond that."

"Luke Casement," said Kate, "has one great fault—if you could call it such. He has an almost fanatical fidelity to any trust. He knows what Jack McCord hoped for, so he's tried to do what old Jack failed at, which was to make a worthwhile man of Yance. But generous as he's been in the matter, there's a limit to Luke's patience. He's stood a lot from Yance, but there'll come a day when Yance will step past the final line. When he does, will he meet up with the hard facts of life!" Kate emphasized her words by clipping the tip from a branch of sage with a hard slash of her whip.

They got back from town at the end of what was, to Sherry at least, another very long day. With her luggage recovered from the Humboldt House and the purchases of a number of things from the Horton and Giles general store, the buckboard was loaded to capacity, and by the time she and Kate had everything carried inside and laid out in some sort of order, the sun was down. Kate refused to stay for supper, insisting she was needed at home. So, with the ranch house filling with the shadows of a quick-flowing dusk, Sherry found herself alone.

She built a fire in the kitchen stove, heated water, and had a good wash. She changed into fresh clothes, then cooked and ate supper in restful solitude. While clearing away the dishes, she heard the outer door of the office open and close. Presently she went in there and found Luke Casement at the desk working on some ranch records. He started to leave his chair, but Sherry waved him back and selected another for herself, settling into it with an unconscious sigh of weariness.

Casement smiled. "A full day, eh?"

"Almost too full," was Sherry's rueful reply. "That Kate Larkin! I never knew such an energetic, capable person. Just trying to keep up with her is really something. She makes me feel rather useless." Sherry told of the crippled steer. "When she did what she had to do, when she shot the poor beast, there was an impression of stern, competent strength."

"Kate will do to take along," Casement said. "You see Dan Vincent at the bank?"

"Yes, and had a long talk with him. I thought him very kind and very wise. He said he was glad I'd decided not to sell the ranch and if I needed help or advice of any kind to come to him about it. I also met a man named Curt Giles in the general store where I bought and bought until I felt guilty. What Kate and I brought back in the buckboard was only part of it. Mr. Giles is sending the rest out tomorrow in a bigger wagon. I'm afraid I ran up an awful bill."

Casement smiled again. "I think the ranch can stand it. You got some riding gear?"

"Yes. And I'm anxious to try it out."

"You'll have the chance. We'll be taking a real ride one of these days."

"Ride to where?"

"Here and there—up and down. Maybe even over past the rim. Every once in a while I take such a jaunt. Call it a sort of survey to get a first-hand look at things. The crew do a pretty good job of keeping their eyes open, but they might not necessarily see what I would."

Sherry studied him. "You're thinking of Milo Hernaman and his threats?"

"That's one angle," Casement admitted.

"I thought I might meet up with him in town," said Sherry soberly. "But I didn't. I did see Francis Quinnault, however. When Kate and I went into the Humboldt House to have lunch with Mrs. Megarry, we were a little late. Francis Quinnault was just leaving. He gave me a funny look and sidled by like he was scared or something."

"The fires of a guilty conscience," observed Casement dryly. "Friend Quinnault got caught with his fingers in the cookie jar. From now on every time he sees you he'll be ready to cut and run."

Silence came as Casement turned back to his bookwork while Sherry fell to musing over the events of the day. More and more slowly moved her thoughts, until they blurred to virtual nothingness. Her head bobbed, and she straightened with a jerk, blinking guiltily, to find Casement regarding her with open amusement.

He chuckled. "Just like a little kid, going to sleep in a chair. About to fall out of it, too. You better go turn in."

Sherry flushed, got up, and marched stiffly to the door. But she paused there and looked over her shoulder, smiling in a softly drowsy way. "My mother always used to say I never did have sense enough to go to bed. Thanks for sending me there."

Alone, Casement considered the door she had closed behind her. A young woman grown, was Sherry Gault—smart and with plenty of spirit. Yet in some ways she was as artless and unspoiled as a child. It would be, he reflected, a matter of regret if various stern tests almost certain to lie ahead should in any way erode that eager, youthful charm. . . .

Weary though she was, Sherry now found sleep maddeningly evasive. She lay wide-eyed and restless, staring up at the dark ceiling. Perhaps she was overtired, or perhaps it was because of the way the events of today and yesterday and the day before kept running about in her mind—things she had seen, things she had heard, people she had met, and the never-ending wonder at the change in her own life and affairs.

Beyond her window the gleam of starlight was added to by an edge of moon lifting past the rim, bringing a steadily increasing glow of silvery light that was at once a lure and a mystery. Pushing aside her blanket, Sherry stole to the window on naked feet. Pale magic drenched the outside world except where poplar trees threw shadows stygian black by contrast. Beyond these shadows the world ran away and away, swimming in a sea of silvery moonfire.

Something stirred at the edge of the tree shadow. Sherry watched, breathless. Was it fact or fancy? Fact, for it came again, movement that resolved into the figure of a man, indistinct, yet distinct enough for certain recognition. Yance Hawn!

She drew swiftly back into the protective darkness of her room. Yance Hawn—out there prowling the night beyond her window! Abruptly she was cold. She caught up a blanket, wrapped herself to the chin, pulled on slippers, and went quietly back through the house to the door of the office. Luke Casement was still in the room beyond that door, for light showed in the crack below the door and she should hear his chair creak as he stirred.

With her hand reaching toward the doorknob, she paused. What on earth was the matter with her? Why should she come running to Casement in this manner? Had he, in the short space of three days, become so important in her life that she must instinctively turn to him at every moment of uncertainty or silly, fancied need? Why the very idea of such a state of affairs was downright ridiculous! Just the same, he was there—within call. . . .

Softly and resolutely she returned to her room and to the window. So far as she could see, the night was now empty of all but its cold, silvery beauty. She got back into bed, grew warm and relaxed, and went to sleep.

Chapter S I X

SHERRY MET the new day eagerly, anticipating all the things she planned to do. She donned a gingham house dress she'd bought in town the day before and while eating breakfast saw Luke Casement and other members of the crew ride away to the south. Soberly, she noted that every man had a scabbarded rifle slung to his saddle. To take her mind off the disturbing significance of this observation, she laid vigorously into the tasks she had set for herself. She heated water, tied a towel about her hair, and began giving the ranch house windows a much-needed washing. Glimpsing her at this, Gabe Tennant came limping over from the cook shack. When Sherry would have sent him back, remarking that it was more important that hardworking cowhands were properly fed, old Gabe shrugged.

"They ain't sufferin' none. They never have suffered on this ranch where good grub and plenty of it is concerned. Besides, I got plenty cooked ahead, as Luke figgered you'd be set to fixin' up the ranch house and would need some help. So let's get at it."

Together they did get at it, with broom, brush,

mop, hot water, and soap. At midmorning the Horton and Giles wagon arrived, and then there were rugs to be put down and several items of furniture brought in and placed. It was a busy day and, for Sherry, a satisfying one, this turning of a relatively barren but staunch old ranch house into a comfortable home. There would be a lot more to be done in the way of window curtains to be hung and paint to be applied in proper colors and proper spots, but she could visualize the final result, and she was content.

Gabe Tennant limped from room to room, nodding his satisfaction. "Left to himself, a male critter is satisfied with mighty little in the way of livin' gear. He just can't be bothered. But you sure got things lookin' good, Missy. All prettied up for a lady to live in. Now if you ain't too tired, there's somethin' else needin' attention."

Amused at the old fellow and already fond of him, Sherry asked, "What's that, Gabe?"

"Learnin' how to handle a gun. Luke said for me to give you a couple of lessons. He said there was a thirty-eight Colt in the office. How's for givin' it a whirl?"

More as a reward for his help than anything else, Sherry agreed. So Gabe got the gun and a box of ammunition from the office cupboard and led the way past the corrals toward the base of the rim. Here he found a rusty old tin dishpan, long discarded. He propped it against a lava boulder, then backed away some fifty feet.

"That'll do. You get so you can hit that three, four times out of six, then you'll be able to take care of yourself."

He showed her how to swing out the cylinder and load the gun. He slapped the cylinder back into place and then all in one movement, so it seemed to Sherry, raised the gun and fired. The bullet rapped into the pan.

"Your turn," Gabe said, and showed her how to grip the gun, aim it, and fire.

Her first attempt was not even close. "That," she said ruefully, "was pretty awful, wasn't it? It wouldn't have hit an elephant."

Gabe's thin laughter cackled. "Shucks, Missy! You closed your eyes and jerked the trigger. But you'll do better, now you've found the gun ain't about to bite you. Jest hold steady as you can, keep your eyes open, and be smooth and easy with the trigger."

Sherry followed instructions as best she could and was rewarded by seeing the bullet strike not far from the pan.

"Better!" Gabe exulted. "Try again."

It took her six more shots before she finally nicked one edge of the pan. Then she missed six times in a row. Yet with every shot she handled the gun with greater confidence. No longer did she fear it. No longer did it feel foreign in her hand or startle her with its recoil. And out of a third cylinder full she hit the pan twice, both times well toward the center.

"That's good enough for today," Gabe decided. "You're gettin' the hang of it. A little more practice and you won't have no trouble lacin' that pan just about every shot."

Sherry looked down at the gun in her hand, her lips pursed. "Do you really think there's any point to it, Gabe? My learning how to shoot this thing, I mean."

"You figger on bein' a real, sure-enough rancher, don't you?" Gabe demanded flatly.

"Yes; of course. But—"

"Then you got to know how to handle a gun. Not jest a six-shooter, but a rifle, too. Cause you never know when you might need to use one or the other. Mebbe you never will. Let's hope so. But should you ever, then nothin' else will do the job. Yes, siree—Missy, you got to be able to handle this six-gun real good and learn how to look straight down the sights of a thirty-thirty, too."

Sherry did not argue the point. It was, she decided, just one more adjustment she had to make if she hoped to fit into the pattern of this Western country.

Later, from her kitchen window, she watched Luke Casement and the rest of the crew ride wearily in through a blue dusk and haul up beside the corrals. She watched them unsaddle and trudge toward the bunkhouse, stamping booted heels to ease the saddle stiffness. She thought of men she had known in the East who, after their day of work in the business world, and though perhaps

115

tired, were still fairly sleek, well turned out, well tailored.

But this was a different world. These men lived closer to the earth and rode through its dust. They looked into the wind and breathed the essence of its freedom and found values there that could not be measured in coin. They were her men; they toiled in her interests. The thought stirred her and made her humble. She would, she vowed, never let them down, never sell them short. If, as Luke Casement had hinted, they stood ready to fight for her, then she would fight for them.

Blue dusk brought with it a comforting sense of contentment. She found herself singing softly as she set about cooking supper. . . .

Later, as she lingered over a second cup of coffee, there came a knock at the kitchen door. Her answering summons brought in Luke Casement. "If I'm a nuisance, throw me out," he said. "Gabe Tennant tells me you've put in a real busy day, so maybe you're too tired to consider that promised ride tomorrow?"

"On the contrary, I can hardly wait." Sherry smiled. "In case you're interested, there's another cup of coffee in the pot." She was quickly up to pour this for him.

"Gabe," she went on, "is an old darling. Between us we did get a lot done. And I can't remember when I've had a more rewarding day. For the first time since arriving here I feel I'm beginning to earn my keep."

He stood with his back to the stove, cup cradled in both hands. Over it, as he lifted it to his lips, his eyes were shadowed with a brooding soberness, and the line of his jaw, Sherry thought, was a trifle grim.

"You," she said, "had a long day of it yourself. Leaving before sunup and not back until dusk. Just out of plain feminine curiosity, is it all right if I ask what you were doing?"

He smiled faintly. "Riding line."

"Riding line . . . ?"

"Patrolling the limits of Clear Creek range. Making sure our cattle—and the other fellow's—stayed where they belong. Make that," he amended with terse vehemence, "that ours do. Where the other fellow's are now, they don't belong."

"Hernaman's?"

"That's right. More Dollar cattle on the Joe Moss range today than the first time the Toland boys saw some there. I'm sending word to Broady Ives in town about it. He knows as well as we do that Hernaman's got no business there, and I'm giving him just a few more days to do something about it. If he doesn't . . . !" Casement shrugged.

"If he doesn't," repeated Sherry slowly, "then we do. Is that it?"

Casement nodded. "We just can't afford to sit still and let Hernaman build up a big herd against our line. Anybody else but him, yes. Because

117

they'd stay there. But not Hernaman. He'll be trying to come across on to Clear Creek land. And if Broady Ives doesn't use that sheriff's star of his for something else than show, I'll make it my business to do something about that, too!"

He drained his cup, put it on the table and moved to the door. "In the morning, then. But not too early."

Sherry went about cleaning up the dishes mechanically. Some of the contentment she had felt was gone. It seemed now as though a sense of invisible pressure had invaded the night.

To get her mind off this, she decided to do something she'd thought of earlier in the day. After all, her decision to embrace a new life in a new land did not mean she should entirely forget the old. Back in the East she had left some good friends who were interested in her welfare and who deserved some kind of assurance that all was well with her. So, from her luggage she collected the necessary materials and settled down at the office desk to write some letters. Certainly she had plenty to write about!

She had finished one letter and was halfway through a second, when the outer door of the office opened and Yance Hawn stepped in. He closed the door and stood with his shoulders squared against it. He looked at her with a sort of predatory speculation, and his teeth shone white as he smiled.

118

"Pretty," he said. "Pretty as a spotted pup. You and me got to become friends. Good friends."

Staring at him, Sherry got quickly to her feet. "You've no business in here," she told him coldly. "I did not ask you in. So you can leave—now!"

He shook his head. "I like this room. I've been in it hundreds of times. Used to sit in here nights and talk with old Jack McCord. Kind of got in the habit of it, and you know how habits are—hard to break? So you and me should do a little visitin'."

There was mockery in his words and mockery in his smile, and he was entirely sure of himself. But to Sherry, despite his good looks he was completely repulsive and preposterous in his conceit.

Abruptly she was stormily angry, and she raked him with scornful, cutting words. "You are an offensive, mannerless fool! Get out!"

Her contempt and scorn struck home. His smile faded, and color rushed strongly to his cheeks. "No you don't," he said roughly. "You can't play that game with me. I know your kind —give a man a come-hither look, then try and back away. I've met your kind before, and I know how to handle them."

He advanced steadily as he spoke and suddenly was right beside her. And she never dreamed of his real intent until it was too late. He caught her by the shoulder and pulled her close, his arms going around her. His lips came down and held hers

119

crushingly. After the first stunned moment of revulsion she fought him desperately, writhing, twisting, kicking. She got a hand up and clawed at his face with raking fingers. But it seemed that nothing could break the vise grip of his arms.

Neither she nor the man who held her heard Luke Casement come in, but suddenly Yance Hawn's grip was torn away and he was sent reeling across the room from a thunderous smash in the mouth. His staggering feet tangled with a chair and he went down in a long sprawl.

Casement moved in on him with cold, toneless words. "You're a rotten, treacherous whelp, Yance. You're no damned good. This is something that's been a long time catching up with you, but it's here now. And you're all through! Get up, damn you—get up!"

Yance Hawn did get up, circling to keep a couple of chairs between him and Casement while he shook off some of the effects of that first savage blow. It hadn't helped his looks any. Already his lips were swollen to a grotesque pout and blood seeped from their corners. But he was heavy in the shoulders, and there was destructive power in him, along with a wild rage.

"I've something for you, too, Casement," he blurted wickedly. "Always I've hated your guts—always!"

A sweep of his hand flung the chairs aside, and he came at Casement with a bounding rush. They

120

met chest to chest with an impact that seemed to shake the room.

For a few long seconds they were virtually motionless, locked in a bitter test of strength. Here, with his heavy shoulders and extra weight, Yance Hawn had an edge, and he began forcing Casement back, inch by stubborn inch. Abruptly Casement gave way, spinning and breaking clear. Unable to check the momentum of his drive, Hawn lurched by. Before he could fully turn and catch his balance again, Casement clubbed him twice under the ear, knocking him floundering through the open doorway into the night.

Shocked and half-stupefied by the upsetting tumult of jangled emotions, Sherry stood frozen, at once frightened, furiously angry, and sick with revulsion. Cold tears flooded her cheeks. Again and again she scrubbed her lips with the back of her hand. She felt besmirched, dirty, nauseated. And the sounds that came back to her through the black rectangle of the doorway were snarling, growling echoes of feral combat, as though they were not human beings out there, but primitive brutes.

Despite her revulsion, her sickness, her scalding anger, she found herself presently at the door, peering out. Movement was there in the night, tangled shapes darker than the dark itself. Human figures rolling on the earth, rearing upright, breaking apart, smashing together again. All these things along with the sound of crushing blows, given and taken.

There was about it all an invisible, malignant fever that reached to touch other men and bring them running from bunkhouse and cook shack. Through the taut calling of their startled voices lifted a shrillness from old Gabe Tennant in strong partisanship for Luke Casement.

How long it went on Sherry did not know. It might have been relatively short moments, or it could have been long minutes. But done it was, finally, and then the voice that came, heavy and drained, belonged to Luke Casement.

"He's heading out—all through here. . . . Put him on a horse. I'll get his time!"

There was further shifting and movement and the growl of voices. Then Casement came back through the office door, smeared with dust and sweat, disheveled, carrying the marks of violence. One sleeve of his sun-faded shirt was torn completely off, and the shirt front was blotched with the crimson of blood, some of this his own, still leaking down his chin from cut and battered lips. Under bruised and darkening brows his eyes still burned with the light of stark, vicious combat. His chest lifted and fell in harsh breathing, and he weaved a trifle as he moved.

He crossed to the corner cupboard and brought out the metal money box. He opened it and tried to count out some of the bills it contained. But for

122

the moment his fingers seemed numbed and clumsy. He turned smoldering eyes on Sherry.

"You do it. Forty dollars. Count it out. Hawn's pay."

She obeyed automatically, and as she laid the money out on the desk, she found herself speaking. "He did not knock. I did not ask him in. He had no right . . . I—I had no idea he would—dare touch me. . . ." Her glance lifted to meet Casement's fairly. "Oh, Luke—I didn't—I didn't . . . !" She half-sobbed the denial.

The bleakness, the lingering harshness of combat in him gave way to something close to gentleness. "Of course you didn't. If I thought otherwise I wouldn't have interfered." He scooped up the money she had counted and moved back into the night.

Reaction settled in. Sherry dropped into a chair and crouched down, choking back a fresh tide of tears, too whipped and miserable even to close the door. This land . . . ! How could she ever call it home? How could she ever hope to know and value it when this sort of thing could happen?

She was still huddled there when Casement returned. He had washed up and donned another shirt, and aside from some swelling at a corner of his mouth and several facial bruises, he showed little visual evidence of what he'd been through. He stood before her and, when she looked forlornly up, showed her the hint of a grave smile.

"A few bad moments, come and gone," he comforted. "Chalk it up to experience. Put it on the profit side of the account. It gave me good reason to get rid of Yance Hawn without feeling I'd short-changed the memory of Jack McCord. So don't look as though the world has come to an end. It hasn't. Tomorrow is another day, and we've some riding to do, remember?"

"How—how can you shrug it off so—so easily?" Sherry whimpered. "To—to me it was awful—just terrible!"

"Call it another rough spot in the trail. You have to climb over such places and keep on going."

Here again, she thought, was the same force she had sensed in Kate Larkin during the crippled steer incident. An indomitable inner fiber . . .

She straightened wearily. "People like you have so much strength—the kind I'm afraid I never will possess."

A flicker of harshness tightened Casement's cheeks. "I didn't have enough to bring myself to kill him. And maybe I should have."

He stared at the wall, then shook himself and turned back to her, his tone once more mild. "Don't worry about your strength and courage. You've more of both than you know. You proved that when you stood up to Milo Hernaman and decided to keep the ranch."

The praise warmed and strengthened her. She

124

managed a wan smile. "I'm sorry I sniveled so. Little by little bit, I'm learning."

Never before had Sherry worn the kind of riding clothes Kate Larkin had helped her select from the shelves of the Horton and Giles store—divided skirt of plain khaki, a blue cotton blouse with neckerchief to match, flat-brimmed Stetson hat with a braided leather chin thong, waist-length fleece-lined jacket, and finally, small hand-stitched half boots. Everyday working clothes, so Kate called them.

After taking a final survey in her wall mirror, Sherry left the ranch house carrying her hat by the chin thong. Her luxuriant black hair was parted in the middle and drawn smoothly back, and the brewing excitement and anticipation that colored her cheeks and put a sparkle in her eyes made her prettier than she knew.

Overhead, morning sunlight flodded past the crest of the rim to gild the western part of the valley and all the world beyond with a fresh brilliance. Here at headquarters, however, the shadow of the rim still held and the air was brisk and cool. Over at the corrals Luke Casement waited with two horses.

"Do I look as strange as I feel?" Sherry asked with some diffidence as she came up to him. "Back home, riding clothes were considerably different from these."

"You look as you should," he told her. "Exactly

125

right." He handed her the reins of a slim-legged little chestnut filly. "Yours. Smart and gentle as a kitten and can run like a windblown shadow should you ever need such speed."

They rode down to the valley floor, out of the rim's shadow and into the pour of the sun. Along a trail paralleling the creek, Casement turned south, setting the pace at an easy jog. Within a couple of miles Sherry sat her saddle with full confidence. Already she was in love with the spirited, easy-gaited little animal under her.

On all sides cattle grazed, sleek and full-bodied. Calves fed at the udders of their mothers or frolicked in the sun. A herd bull, massive and seemingly half-asleep, stood in solitary dignity. From a little swale a flock of sage hens flushed and sailed off to some further covert and once, where the willows thinned out to disclose a long creek pool shining silver in the sun. A pair of mallard ducks whipped into startled flight, the drake's head scintillating like a green jewel. Out of the very earth itself there seemed to lift a primitive wine of vigor that held Sherry fascinated and breathless.

She swung the little filly closer to the big grullo Casement was riding.

"Almost," she cried, "it's as if last night never happened at all."

Casement nodded, smiling. "That's the spirit. I told you there was always a new day coming up to count on."

She twisted in her saddle, looking all around her. "We're still on Clear Creek land?"

"Not even close to leaving it," he assured her.

In time they came into a harsher area, a land of lava outcrop where the grass ran thin and stunted sagebrush stood scattered. A branch trail led into it, and Casement took that way. The lava outcrop ran into a blunt-nosed finger ridge that reached back toward the face of the rim and lifted toward its crest.

The way steepened, and Casement, who up to now had ridden with a loose and casual ease, began leaning forward and peering down past the grullo's off shoulder at the run of the trail ahead. Presently, where the steepness of the ridge eased enough to allow a shallow shelf of earth-drift to form and hold, he hauled up and dismounted, to survey the trail at even closer range. He climbed the steady rise of the ridge a good hundred yards on foot, leading the grullo, with his head bent and his glance intent. When he finally swung into the saddle again there was no longer any careless ease in him, but instead an air of hawkishness as his glance lifted and reached for the nearing crest of the rim.

Sherry had watched all this maneuvering and wondered about it, but not until the panting horses finished their scrambling climb to this rim top did she find room to draw even with her companion and survey her surroundings.

From below and at distance, the rim had the appearance of being flat on top, but it was actually broken and uneven. Conifer timber marched in files along the ridges, with brush browse cloaking the short slopes, and where the sun sifted down across the small flats, grass was beginning to ripen and cure.

Here a vast stillness held, a silence so complete it made Sherry half-afraid to speak. When she did, she unconsciously lowered her voice.

"What," she asked, "did you see along the trail that interested you so?"

"Sign," Casement told her briefly. "Cattle sign. Fresh. Too fresh. Likewise, fresh horse tracks."

"That is unusual?"

"Just now the cattle sign is, because cattle don't leave the valley grass and climb up here unless driven, and we're a full month away from moving any Clear Creek stuff up to summer range. Somebody's been rushing the season, and I wonder why." He tried to make it sound casual, but Sherry did not miss the strong undertone of concern.

His next words really startled her. "Do you think you could find your way back to headquarters alone?"

She stared at him. "Of course. But why should I? Where are you going?"

"Further along. Country gets rougher there. Too rough for you to tackle without more experience."

"Bosh!" exclaimed Sherry flatly. "That, Luke Casement, is the poorest excuse I ever heard. If I could ride up the trail to get here, then I can ride anywhere, and you know it. It's not the country, but what we might find in it that concerns you, isn't it?"

He shrugged resignedly. "Very well. As I said, no cattle of ours drift up here by themselves; somebody drove them. Whoever did could be ready to make an argument about it if caught with the goods. And that would be no sort of an affair for you to mix in."

"You're hinting of thieves—rustlers?"

"That's a word for it."

"Milo Hernaman's work?"

Casement shook his head. "Doubt it. When Hernaman steals, he steals big. Like the way he's working to gobble up the Joe Moss range before having his try at doing the same with us. Not over half a dozen head came up that trail, which makes it more likely the work of some small-time outfit."

Sherry had another look around. Here the clean, towering boles of the ponderosa pines shone warm and brown where the sun struck through. Never, she thought, had she glimpsed a more peaceful world. Yet there was the evidence Casement had seen along the trail—and his explanation gave the lie to this seeming peacefulness.

"If things are as you say, Luke, where would the cattle be driven to?"

"Heading for the Meridian Creek country, most likely. There are some wildcat mines working there, any of them glad to eat cheap beef without worrying about where it came from."

"And what have you in mind?"

"Run the sign down and see where it goes."

"Very well," Sherry said determinedly. "Let's see where it goes. Lead out. I'm going with you."

Her head was up, her chin set, her glance direct. Casement nodded. "Very well. We'll run it down together, for a way, at least. But should we meet up against something that doesn't look good to me, then you'll do as you're told, and no argument. Understand?" The words were blunt and stern.

"Maybe," she retorted with rising spirit. "And maybe I should remind you who you're speaking to."

"No need," he said curtly. "I know. To you. The owner of Clear Creek. My boss. But while I ramrod the outfit, I look after all its interests. All of them! Which includes the owner. When I think she should be stood in the corner, that is where she's put! Now, if that's understood, we'll move along. Well . . . ?"

With the wisdom of her sex, Sherry knew when to retreat. "You know where you're going and I don't. So I'll do as I'm told."

They moved out, and Casement hauled his Winchester from the saddle boot and balanced

130

the rifle across the saddle in front of him, handy for instant use if the need arose. For the most part the cattle sign threaded from one twisting flat to another, only on occasion crossing some ridge through the timber where the deep mat of pine needles and other forest duff under foot enabled the horses to move with little sound save a gusty breathing and the sibilant creak of saddle leather.

Not once did Casement look back. All his faculties were intent on probing ahead for what might be there. They dipped through more flats and climbed other ridges, and then, suddenly, at the crest of another ridge, Casement reined abruptly in.

Softly he said, "Smell it? Wood smoke."

Coming up beside him, Sherry caught the acrid odor instantly. A ripple of feeling went up her spine, and she looked around with a touch of unease. "Don't—don't tell me I have to wait here alone," she murmured.

He did not answer, and so, when he stirred the grullo to movement again, Sherry kept pace.

Now the way led downward, through thinning timber. Within fifty yards, Casement reined in again. Close ahead the timber gave way to an open space past a scant fringe of chokecherry. Beyond that the slope became a fairly extensive flat curving off to the left. At the head of it was a small thicket of silver-barked quaking aspen. Below the aspens, the stronger green of the grass told of a

131

water seep, the lower end of this leading into a rough brush corral that held five head of red-flanked, white-faced Hereford cattle.

Off to one side a nondescript roan horse was on picket, and at the edge of the aspens the dying embers of a campfire still sent up a thin, slanting drift of smoke. At one side of the fire lay a saddle and a tangle of blankets and a dirty canvas tarp. Across the fire from these a man hunkered on his heels, alternately picking at bacon in a frying pan and gulping coffee straight from a blackened pot.

Casement went noiselessly out of his saddle and handed the grullo's reins to Sherry. "Stay put until I call," he murmured.

Her heart thumping, her breath rising faster in her throat, Sherry watched as Casement slid, Indian-quiet, out of the timber and past the choke-cherry thickets. Once he was in the complete clear, his voice rang with a quick, hard authority.

"Hold it, Shag! There's a thirty-thirty looking right at you!"

Chapter SEVEN

SHERRY CLEARLY heard the man's blurted exclamation of surprise. His head swung, and he moved as though to surge to his feet, but dropped

132

back at Casement's further harsh order and crouched there motionless save for his swinging, frightened glance.

Moving in swiftly, Casement scooped up a belt and holstered six-shooter from the tangle of blankets. Then he called, "All right, Sherry!"

She rode down to the flat, leading the grullo. Casement indicated his prisoner. "Meet Shag Buckholt. Once a Clear Creek hand. But too lazy and whiskey-hungry for even big-hearted, tolerant Jack McCord to stand for very long. Now, apparently, he's out on his own in a big way. What you got to say for yourself, Shag?"

"Only that I don't savvy this, you comin' in on me this way with a Winchester—just like you figgered you were roundin' up some kind of damn outlaw." The words were sulky and aggrieved.

"Maybe I'm doing just that," Casement charged. "What about those five beef critters in the corral yonder?"

Buckholt shrugged. "All right, what about 'em? Why don't you ask Yance Hawn. They belong to him."

"Belong to Hawn! Who says so?"

Buckholt shrugged again. "He does. He drove 'em in here. I'm just workin' for him—keepin' an eye on them for him until he can get away long enough to drive 'em over to some feller in the Meridian Crick country who wants to buy 'em. Yance figgered he might be able to make it today, and

133

I'm sure hopin' so, as I'm gettin' plenty fed up with hangin' around here by myself."

Casement scoffed. "Try again, Shag. You can think up a better one. Yeah, you'll have to lie faster than that if you figure to make a real success at rustling."

"Rustlin'!" The word fairly leaped from Buckholt. "Who said anything about rustlin'? I ain't about to rustle nothin' from nobody. Hell, man! You think I'm out to get my neck stretched? I tell you I'm jest workin' for Yance Hawn—helpin' him with some of his own cows. And that's all I'm doin'."

Casement studied him from under frowning brows.

"You'd try and tell me Yance Hawn drove five head of Clear Creek beef up here and claimed they were his own? You gone so blind you can't read a brand that I can see from here? Your eyes turned that bad?"

"Ain't a thing wrong with my eyes," Buckholt defended. "So help me, it's like I told you. Yance said this little jag of stuff was the first of fifty head Jack McCord left him when he died."

"And you believed him?"

" 'Course. Why shouldn't I? I recollect how— when I was ridin' for Clear Creek—old Jack used to treat Yance kind of extra special. Seemed so to me he did. So when Yance told me what he did, I figgered—well, that's the way it was."

Casement condidered for another frowning

134

moment. "That," he said grudgingly, "sounds almost loco enough to be true." He put his glance on Sherry. "What do you think?"

She had been watching Buckholt closely. He was a lank, gangling sort with a long, narrow face, a weak chin, and restless, worried eyes. He was, on snap judgment, a pretty poor specimen of humanity, but she did feel he was telling the truth.

"I think it is as he says, Luke. I'm recalling that Yance Hawn had been up here past the rim for the purpose—according to him—of trying to run down and rope a wild horse. But when I asked him if he'd caught one he acted rather queer and shifty."

"Just so," Casement agreed. Again he faced Buckholt. "When did Hawn bring the cattle in, Shag?"

Buckholt calculated, lips moving as he counted off on his fingers.

"Four days ago," he announced. "Me, I been up here longer than that—nearer ten days. Met up with Yance in town one night. He bought me a couple of bottles, staked me to some grub, and told me to come up here, make a camp, and wait for him to show with his stock. Which I did. But if them cows yonder are really stolen stuff, I never knew it until now, and I want no part of 'em."

"Don't worry, you won't get any," Casement told him. "Friend Yance has been feeding you tall talk, Shag. He's no claim to a single head of Clear Creek beef; Jack McCord never left him

135

even the hide of one. Likewise and besides, he's no longer riding for Clear Creek. He was fired last night. I think the best thing you can do is clear out—go a long way from any part of this range. Because should I ever find you fooling around with any more Clear Creek cattle, it will be awful hard for me to believe you, no matter what your story."

"I'll clear out," promised Buckholt eagerly. "Damn right I will. And should I ever meet up with Yance Hawn again I'll read him off, plenty!"

"Best not, Shag," Casement told him dryly. "He might turn rough. When he does, he can be a pretty mean character. I know. So roll your gear and get started."

He unloaded Buckholt's gun and dropped it on the blankets. Then he stood aside and watched while Buckholt hurriedly brought in his horse, threw on the saddle, packed his gear, and stepped into the leather.

"Make it any direction you prefer, Shag," was Casement's parting instruction. "Just so it is away from here."

Sherry watched Buckholt disappear into the timber. She looked at Casement and spoke simply. "He was telling the truth, Luke—I'm sure of it. I'm glad you let him go."

"All right with me if it is with you." Casement nodded. "Now let's start moving the cattle back where they belong."

He tore away a portion of the makeshift brush

corral, freeing the five whitefaces. They immediately began feeding across the green of the water seep. Casement pointed at the closest animal.

"Can you figure out the brand?"

Sherry studied the stamp marking on the slope of the critter's near haunch. "I'm guessing, of course," she said slowly, "but to me it looks like two squashed-in squares, side by side."

Casement chuckled. "Not bad. Couldn't you call it a Double Diamond?"

"Of course! Exactly so. A Double Diamond. That is my—our regular brand?"

"Officially registered," said Casement. "Any four-legged critter you see hereabouts packing that iron is yours—Clear Creek property." With a bite of grimness he added, "Looks like Yance Hawn doesn't believe that. So the book isn't closed on him yet."

He stepped into the saddle and swung the grullo in a short turn that bunched the cattle and started them toward the timber. One of them, hungry from confinement and reluctant to leave the grass along the water seep, tried to dodge back. Of its own accord, Sherry's little filly mount blocked the maneuver neatly.

Once lined out through the timber, the stock moved along at a fair pace, only here and there snatching a mouthful of grass. For Sherry, it was a brand-new experience—riding a horse of her own, driving cattle of her own, across wild range of her own. It all seemed incredible in the light of what her life had been a short week or two before. But now—it was true! . . .

By the time they got the stock back to the edge of the rim and started down the ridge trail to the valley below, the morning hours had run away.

Casement hauled up on the crest. "They'll make it on their own, now. And we might as well make good use of what Gabe Tennant fixed up for us. Hungry, maybe?"

"Now that you mention it, yes," Sherry admitted. "You mean you have food along?"

"Some. So, as the old saying goes—light and rest your saddle. Just let the reins trail. The filly won't go far."

Free of the saddle, Sherry stretched and took in the surroundings. The midday sun was baking out the resin breath of the pines, and the still air was charged with the richness of it. Perched on a lava ledge she alternated in looking over the far miles of the world below and watching Luke Casement as he built a tiny fire and, from a roll of canvas tied behind his saddle cantle, produced a battered coffeepot, a couple of equally battered tin cups, and a package of cold steaks and biscuits. He poured water from a canteen into the pot, added a handful of coffee, and set the pot on the fire. Soon it was steaming, and the coffee fragrance drew Sherry over to it.

"Suddenly I'm ravenous," she proclaimed.

He poured the coffee, settled back on his heels, and showed her a small grin of satisfaction that was almost boyish. "One of life's better moments. Simple food for simple hunger. Dig in!"

They ate with gusto, holding cold steak in their fingers and biting off pieces of it, and they drank deep of the strong black coffee.

"Gorgeous!" Sherry mumbled. "Just gorgeous. If I'm acting the pig, it's because I can't help it. I never tasted anything even half so good."

With the last crumb gone she licked her fingers shamelessly and suddenly laughed aloud.

Casement eyed her, wondering.

"It's me I'm laughing at," she explained. "Seeing myself as I was once and as I am now. I thought my other life was good. . . ."

She had taken off her hat, and where a probing shaft of sunlight touched it, her hair took on the glossy sheen of a blackbird's wing. Her blue eyes were crystal-clear and her cheeks smooth and warm with color, and in any man's eyes at this moment, she was a vivid, lovely thing. Meeting Casement's glance, she read in it his judgment of this, and abruptly her laughter was gone, replaced by a breathless stillness that grew and grew. . . .

Thin and flat with distance, sound of the shot came up from the valley below. Two more followed it quickly, and they brought Casement to his feet and to the rim's edge, his glance roaming and probing the land below.

"One shot doesn't necessarily mean anything," he said tersely, "but three of them . . . ! Let's get down there!"

He stamped out the fire, rolled up his gear, mounted, and set the grullo onto the fast-descending trail. Keeping pace behind, Sherry found the descent a more trying journey than the upward climb had been. By the time they reached the flats, the muscles of her legs were trembling from the strain of forward pressure, and the jolting of the filly's sliding, scrambling descent had loosened her hair until it hung about her shoulders.

Ahead of her, Casement stood high in his stirrups, one arm thrown up. Across the distance a man standing by one of the creek's willow thickets answered the gesture, and Casement, touching the grullo with the spurs, went forward at a slashing run.

The little filly was not to be left behind. Then and there Sherry found that when Casement spoke of a fleeting shadow, he had used the right words. Wind roared in her ears and whipped her eyes until they streamed. Her hat fell back between her shoulders, and only the chin thong, tugging at her throat, kept her from losing it. The movement was violent, beating the very breath from her; yet it was thrilling smooth and sure, and she knew no fear, only a stirring exultation.

The run ended as abruptly as it had started, with the filly dancing restlessly and eager for more of the same. Sherry cleared her eyes with a sleeve and saw that the man by the willows was Griff Toland. He carried a rifle and limped slightly as he came forward to meet Casement. His face was dark with anger and strain. He jerked his head toward the willows.

"Lee's in there, Luke. We got to get him home. They shot him, Luke. Yance Hawn—may God forever damn his worthless soul—him and Pete Hugo, that foreman of Hernaman's—they shot Lee and killed our broncs! . . ."

Casement was instantly down, following Griff Toland into the willows. Held for a dumbfounded moment, Sherry slid from her saddle and ran after them.

Lee Toland lay on a patch of sand close to the rippling creek waters. The right side of his shirt was dark and wet with a crimson stain. Casement and Griff bent over him and began opening his shirt. Hardly understanding her own moves, Sherry pushed in beside them.

"Let me!" She peeled back the soggy shirt. The wound was a ragged tear, high up on the right side below the armpit. Warm blood welled from it. Sherry whipped off her neckerchief, soaked it in the cold creek water, and began carefully cleansing the wound.

Lee Toland stared up at her with eyes glazed with shock and pain, and protested weakly. "Not for you to do, ma'am. No need you get on your knees like this. No need you get blood on your hands. I'll make it all right—I'll make it . . . !"

"Of course you'll make it," Sherry assured him gently. "We'll get you home. But first we must do what we can here. And," she added, "if I can't stand the blood of one of my own men on my hands—then I deserve nothing—nothing!"

While she worked she listened to Griff Toland explain to Casement, "Lee and me, we'd been down along our south line to see if any of our cows had drifted that far durin' the night. None had, but we picked up sign showin' mebbe ten or a dozen head of stock had come in off the Joe Moss range and were leadin' up the west side of the creek. We couldn't figger this, so followed along. We caught up with them at the old Bondurant Crossing. There was ten head of Hernaman's stuff, and Yance Hawn and Pete Hugo were drivin' 'em.

"What they were aimin' to do or exactly where they were goin', Lee and me didn't have time to find out. Minute we came in sight, Hawn drew a gun and knocked Lee out of the saddle. Then Pete Hugo cut loose and dropped my horse. The bronc went out from under me so quick I got caught by one leg, and before I could get untangled and hold of my Winchester they dropped Lee's horse and hauled out, hell-bent, back down stream. They musta figgered some other Clear Creek hands were close, or else they might have taken time to finish me off. Anyhow, they lit out. I lugged Lee over here to the creek then happened to see you comin' down off the rim. And like I say, I can't figger what Hawn and Pete Hugo were up to."

"We'll look for the answer to that later," Casement said. "Right now Lee's our worry."

Sherry rinsed out her neckerchief again, wrung

142

it partially, and made a cold, wet compress to put over the wound. To Casement she said, "That flour sack Gabe put our lunch in—get it!"

With Casement helping, she tore the sack in strips and bandaged the compress tightly in place. With the first edge of shock easing somewhat, Lee Toland managed a weak, white-lipped smile.

"That's fine, ma'am—just fine. Now if somebody'll just help me on a horse . . ."

Between them, Casement and Griff put him on the big grullo. Casement untied the pack behind the cantle and tossed it aside. He swung up behind the wounded rider, steadying him with an encircling arm. He looked at Sherry. "Griff will ride with you. The filly can pack double."

That was the way they went home, back along the grim, anxious miles. As she rode, it came to Sherry with the sharpest clarity and conviction what she must do—what she would do. Owning a ranch was one thing—being worthy of it was something else. It wasn't enough to sit back and let others fight and bleed and perhaps die for you. Woman or no, you couldn't settle for that, or you'd never be able to live with yourself. There were ways in which even a woman might fight, and that would be her way.

When they finally climbed the slope to headquarters, Kate Larkin's pony was tied at the corrals and Kate herself showed at the door of the cook shack. As Casement reined the grullo to a stop at the bunkhouse, with Lee Toland sagging drained and white against his supporting arm, Kate came running.

Griff Toland dropped off from in back of Sherry, lifted his brother down, and carried him into the bunkhouse. Following close at his heels, Kate Larkin showed the strongest expression of stricken regret and worry Sherry had ever witnessed.

Limping hurriedly from the cook shack, Gabe Tennant sent shrill call ahead. "What's wrong—what's wrong?"

"Plenty!" Casement told him bleakly. He looked at Sherry as she slid to the ground. "You'll rake up something for clean bandages?"

"Yes." She paused before turning away. "Something I want understood. Don't you do anything about this, or allow any of our men to do anything, until you've talked it out with me. That is the way I want it. That, if I must put it so, is an order!"

Narrow-eyed, Casement studied her for a moment, then nodded. "Very well," he said.

Sherry hurried into the ranch house for the necessary clean cloth. She was returning with some when Kate Larkin came from the cook shack with a bucket of steaming water. Kate's eyes were moist, and her lips trembled when she spoke. "If —if Lee should die—I'll never, never forgive myself. Sometimes, Sherry Gault, we women can be such fools—such silly fools!"

In the bunkhouse Luke Casement and Griff Toland had Lee between blankets and Gabe Tennant was holding a whiskey flask to the wounded man's lips. Lee gagged a little, and Kate Larkin snatched the flask away.

"Oh, Gabe—you and your old whiskey!" she scolded. "Do you want to strangle him? Get away and let me work!"

She removed the old compress. Peering past her shoulder, Sherry saw that the wound had ceased to bleed, but it lay raw and angry-looking.

"That," said Kate without looking up, "needs stitches to close it up, and I'm not that good. Somebody go get Doc Aden."

"Right away," Griff Toland said, starting for the door.

"Take my saddle, Griff," Casement called. "Put it on that belted Idaho roan we brought in last year. It's a hard-mouthed brute but has more long-range running in it than any horse on the ranch."

Kate Larkin took over completely. "I'm staying right here," she announced. "This man needs quiet, so the rest of you can leave."

Thus dismissed, Gabe Tennant limped out with his whiskey flask, vowing that whiskey and chewing tobacco in good supply had healed more than one man, and for his money were as good as, or better than, a lot of new-fangled stuff. Besides, he added grumbling, when some women got worked up they could be just too damn bossy.

Kate paid him no attention. She was crooning softly, and her eyes were luminous as she got a fresh bandage in place. Catching Sherry's eye,

145

Casement nodded toward the door. They went softly out.

"That," Casement said as they reached the open, "seems to have straightened out one matter. Our Katie has learned herself a lesson, even though the cure it took is pretty severe."

"Lesson?" Sherry murmured.

"Just so. Such as that while you may lead a man a considerable distance without him setting back on the halter rope, there's generally a limit on how far you can drive him. So now Katie is ready to take Lee exactly as he is, instead of trying to make him into something else before agreeing to marry him."

"So-o!" exclaimed Sherry softly. "That is how it is, eh? Now I understand why she looked—as she did. And what she meant."

Up on the Idaho roan, Griff Toland raced away along the town trail. Casement looked after him soberly. "A good man, that. He and Lee have always been close as brothers go, liking to ride together, looking out for each other. Just now all he can think of is making sure Lee will pull through all right. Afterward, he's apt to be a little hard to hold back where Yance Hawn and Pete Hugo are concerned. The same goes for Sam Kell and Al Birch. For that matter, it goes for me, too."

"That," said Sherry, "is exactly what I want to talk to you about." She led the way over to the ranch house. Afternoon warmth lay close and heavy along the earth. The sun struck up glint-

146

ing flashed on the nearer face of the rim and clouded the further run of it in a coiling blue haze. Down in the green, water-fed creek meadows, cattle worked slowly in to drink, then rested in the thin shade of the willows. Just the faintest up-draft of air came in off the flats and climbed the face of the rim, and its passing stirred the leaves of the poplar trees to a shimmering whisper.

In the cool shadow of the office Sherry took off her hat, tossed it on the desk, then tidied her hair a bit with deft fingers—fingers that had, but a lit-tle time ago, been stained with the blood of a faith-ful rider. She was thinking of that as she dropped into a chair, and the thought served to strengthen her determined intentions.

"What," she asked, looking up at Casement, "do you think was the purpose of the Dollar cattle being driven onto our range by Yance Hawn and that—what's his name?—that Pete Hugo? Ac-cording to Griff Toland, this man Pete Hugo is a foreman of Milo Hernaman's. What would he and Yance Hawn be doing riding together, and what was their purpose?"

Casement tipped a shoulder. "I can speculate, that's all. It doesn't—or wouldn't—surprise me if Hawn has gone over to Hernaman. Being the kind he is, he's bound to try and get even in some way. Maybe Hernaman had him and Pete Hugo move that little bunch of Dollar beef onto our range to test our reactions. If we stood for it with-out hitting back quick and hard, then he'd move in some more to get a solid foothold. If we did hit back—well, the issue was bound to come to a showdown sooner or later. So why not now?"

He considered for a moment before offering a second possibility. "Maybe Hawn had ideas of running some Dollar beef across the rim like he did ours, and talked Pete Hugo into the deal with him. Which would be no occasion for surprise, as Pete is hardly what you'd call one of our better citizens. He wouldn't be above collecting an extra dollar or two, even if he had to double-cross or steal from the man paying him wages. And you saw how thick-headed Shag Buckholt could be. Hawn wouldn't have any trouble selling him some wild yarn on how he happened to get hold of the Dollar cattle. So there are my two ideas on that deal. But," he added shrewdly, "that's not the main thing you wanted to talk about."

Sherry stood up and began pacing about the room. "No, it's not. What concerns me most is what came to me when I saw Lee Toland lying there at the edge of the creek with that strained, shocked pain and numbness in his eyes. I knew then that there were certain things I must do and certain things I must not allow others to do. I realized then that I could not sit back and let men like you and Lee and Griff take all the risks, do all the fighting, while I sat at home in safety, risking nothing. I knew that if I was fit only for that, then I was not entitled to own this ranch or any other.

I knew I had to share the risk and share the fight.

"Being what I am, I can't take up a gun as a man might. But there are other means. I will fight with what I have, with whatever money this ranch represents. Down to the last cent, if necessary. I will also, if necessary, hire the best lawyer I can find to carry our case to the highest court in the land. I'll see that the truth is laid before people who count, even the Governor of the state if it must be that way. I don't care where Milo Hernaman's influence reaches or how far; I'll challenge it and see if it is as strong as some people think."

She paused in her pacing and faced him. "Tomorrow, Luke, you and I go to town, where I will talk with a number of people. I want you along to—shall we say—back my hand." She showed him a small, grave smile. "I hope you don't think I'm just a scatter-wit, dreaming of miracles."

During the time it took to roll and light a cigarette he did not answer. Then he met her glance fairly. "Of course not. Maybe Hernaman can be handled that way. We'll at least give it a try. And what do I think? I think Jack McCord would be very proud of you and that the folks in the East lost something extra special when they let go of you!"

Color flooded strongly into her cheeks as she moved over to the inner door and opened it. "Now you're guessing," she retorted defensively, to cover her confusion. "I'll probably turn out much too weak to finish what I start. And perhaps I am looking for a miracle. But I must have my try at it. Now I'm going to clean up and give Kate a hand—if she'll let me."

Chapter   E I G H T

RETURNING TO THE bunkhouse, Casement stopped beside Kate Larkin. She had pulled a chair up to Lee Toland's bunk and was sitting quietly, holding one of his hands in both of hers, watching him as though she could thus lend him some of her own splendid strength. Lee lay quiet, his breathing regular, a tinge of color back in his drawn cheeks.

Casement touched Kate on the shoulder. "He's a good man, Katie—and you're not going to lose him."

Kate nodded, her eyes misting.

Lee's eyes opened, and he smiled faintly. "Don't reckon I'll ever be good enough to deserve Kate, but I sure aim to try. And Luke—I got a ninety-dollar saddle cinched on a dead bronc, down at the Bondurant Crossing. I can't afford to lose that hull."

"You're not going to," Casement told him. "I'm heading after it now—your gear and Griff's. So rest easy, boy."

He went out and caught up and harnessed a team to the buckboard. Griff Toland had taken his saddle for the run to town but had stripped it of the scabbarded Winchester that had been strapped to it, thus lightening the roan's load by that much. Now Casement slung the gun behind the buckboard seat.

He drove down through the meadows, crossed the creek at the regular ford, and turned south. Here were no roads, and the way was rough, but wheels had rolled over it before when Jack McCord, too infirm physically in his waning years to climb in and out of a saddle, had traveled over much of the ranch by buckboard.

Casement's thoughts returned to Sherry Gault and her stated plan of defense against Milo Hernaman. It was an understandable reaction on the part of a gently reared, compassionate girl at having a man shot down in defense of her interests, and she did not want it happening again. Admirable as the sentiment was, however, in Casement's sober judgment it stood little chance against such as Milo Hernaman—the man was too shrewd, too ruthless, with a power that reached too far both financially and politically.

It did not matter that Hernaman had few if any friends, that he was undoubtedly hated by a hundred men where he was tolerated by one; this would bother him not at all. He would probably find such a condition actually to his advantage, for being hated by many meant being feared by many, and such fear made for power. You stood up to men like Hernaman successfully only if you turned their own weapons on them, and did it just as ruthlessly.

Casement had no trouble finding the scene of the shooting. The horses lay as they had fallen, close to the creek cover but in the open. A number of buzzards were hovering, though none had actually settled on the carcasses. He took a good and careful look around before reining his team into a break in the willows where they and the rig were partially concealed. Then, rifle in hand, he began prowling the creek, up and down, stirring cattle into movement.

Presently he found what he was looking for, ten head that were still roughly bunched, all carrying Milo Hernaman's Dollar brand. This was assurance enough that Yance Hawn and Pete Hugo had not come back.

He returned to the dead horses and stripped the gear from them, viewing the stricken animals with regret. Good, sound saddle stock they had been, but now just carrion, cruelly wasted. He piled the recovered gear in the buckboard, backed the rig clear, and circled to the east side of the creek by way of the Bondurant Crossing. There he collected the few items of gear he'd left when taking Lee Toland up on the grullo.

By this time the afternoon was well along and shadows were beginning to form. Round about

152

lay a land he had looked across many, many times before, and now, as always, it furnished him with a sense of fullness and satisfaction. For there was in him the capacity to savor a land's free gifts of distance and substance and color, and these things always served to strengthen and renew him. A man's days, he mused, might be filled with the monotony of his labors, but there was much to reward him if he looked about him with proper perception.

At headquarters Al Birch and Sam Kell were prowling back and forth, grim and restless. Their day of work had kept them at the upper end of the ranch, and only lately had they learned from Gabe Tennant what had happened. They came over to give Casement a hand at unhitching the buckboard team, and Sam Kell made harsh demand.

"When are we goin' to take care of that fellow Hernaman, Luke? When are we goin' to back him into a corner and finish him? He's already lived too long—hurt too many people."

"That may come," Casement countered. "But not until I give the word. Hernaman might have been behind this particular deal, and then again he might not. The only thing we know for sure is that a jag of Dollar cows showed on our land, with Yance Hawn and Pete Hugo driving them. And it was Hawn who cut down on our boy Lee."

"Hawn!" spat Al Birch, usually the most quiet and contained of men. "I never did like or trust that fellow. Too slick—too smooth. So now he's gone over to Hernaman, eh? Luke, you should have broke his damn neck last night instead of just whipping hell out of him and firing him!"

Sam Kell scrubbed a thoughtful hand across his jaw. "You say Hawn and Pete Hugo drove some Dollar beef onto our land. They wouldn't have done that unless Hernaman ordered it."

"Doesn't seem so," Casement admitted. "But they had the cattle at the Bondurant Crossing, and that's just about dead opposite the trail that leads up to the rim."

"Yeah," grunted Sam Kell puzzled. "So it is. But does that mean anything special?"

"Maybe." Casement sketched briefly what he and Sherry Gault had run across up past the rim. "And," he finished, "Shag Buckholt swore up and down that Yance Hawn claimed the cows were part of fifty head Jack McCord had left him in his will."

"So-o!" growled Kell. "Now we find friend Hawn was—along with everything else—just a mangy cow thief, stealin' from his hire. That was what he was up to while claiming he was after a wild horse. You figure that him and Pete Hugo were set to run that jag of Dollar beef across the rim too? Hugo's the sort to sell out his own outfit if he figgered he could make it stick."

"Call it a thought," Casement said. "I'm driving Miss Gault to town tomorrow—at her order.

154

She has an idea she wants to try out. While she's working at it, I'll try and locate Hernaman and ask him some straight questions. Maybe I'll find out about Pete Hugo and Yance Hawn."

"Me," said Al Birch, "I want to meet up with Mr. Hawn. Then we'll see—we'll see . . . !"

"First things first," warned Casement. "Right now the main thing is for Doc Aden to get here, fix up Lee, and give us the real word on him."

It was after dark when Doc Aden rolled up to Clear Creek headquarters in a livery rig, followed closely by Griff Toland on the now weary Idaho roan. Casement tied Doc's team for him and carried his bag into the bunkhouse, where Sherry Gault and Kate Larkin had been waiting out the anxious hours together.

Doctor George Aden was a slender man with angular features and alert blue eyes. His thinning hair was gray about the temples, and his manner was brusk but kindly. He had served a long time in this back country at the edge of the desert and was no stranger to gunshot wounds and other marks of violence. Also, he had learned that the feuds and conflicts and antagonisms of one sort or another that accounted for such injuries were not necessarily his affair, so he seldom inquired as to the how or why. His main job, as he saw it, was to mend, if possible, what other men had sought to destroy, and to that end he bent his full energy and wisdom.

He returned all greetings perfunctorily and got quickly to work, washing up, then baring the wound.

Lee Toland looked up at him with fever-brightened eyes. "Ain't too much, Doc. Just a scrape along the ribs. Hate to be so much bother. . . ."

Doc spoke to no one in particular.

"Just why fool humans try to make light of things like this I'll never know. Yet for some reason they generally do." To Lee directly he added, "My boy, if that slug had dug half an inch deeper, it would have got hold of a rib and torn out half of your chest. As it is, you're far from being hale and hearty, and I see fever in your eyes. So don't talk; lie still and hang on—because I'm going to hurt you. Not because I want to, but because I have to. Yes, hurt you. Not as much as I've had to hurt others—but some. Now if I could have this lamp a little closer, and another to this side . . . ?"

They placed the lamps as Doc directed, and he went to work again.

They saw Lee stir convulsively in the blankets, heard the quick, hard catch of his breath as Doc began doing what had to be done, sewing up the wound. Lee sweated and groaned, and tried to hold out. But there were too many of those necessary stitches, and abruptly he went still and limp, and Kate let out a small wail.

"Docter—he's . . . !"

"Fainted," supplied Doc Aden cheerfully.

"Which is all to the good. Now I can really pull things together. Time he gets his wits back, the job will be done."

"Somebody did a fine job of cleaning up that wound, which always helps," went on Doc Aden as he finished and turned. "With a thing of this sort it is so often the infection that raises hell—if you ladies don't mind me putting it that plainly. This lad here has some fever, which is to be expected, though nothing to worry about unless it gets much higher. And we'll keep an eye out for that."

To Casement he added, "Luke, you'll have to find a bunk for me. I'm just not up to driving home tonight. I've had a long day of it. When Griff caught up with me I'd just got back to town from Barney Coheen's place out at Rubicon Flat, where I brought another Nevada citizen squalling into the world. And I haven't eaten in twelve hours."

"Then you soon will, Doctor, over at the ranch house," said Sherry quickly. "Just as soon as I can get supper together. You, too, Kate."

"Right!" approved Doc heartily, taking Kate by the arm. "Lee will still be here when you get back; he's not going anywhere for several weeks."

They ate supper, and Kate lingered long enough to help with the dishes, then headed back to the bunkhouse. Sitting at ease with his pipe and a final cup of coffee, Doc Aden made smiling remark as he watched her leave. "Quite a girl, Kate Larkin."

"She's wonderful!" exclaimed Sherry, drying

157

her hand on her apron and taking a chair across the table from Doc. "She's very capable—very strong."

Doc smiled again. "I understand you're a pretty stout character yourself. On the way out from town, Griff Toland filled me in on several things. For a tenderfoot—and I say that admiringly—you did pretty well for yourself when you gave Lee first-aid."

Sherry's laugh was small and deprecating. "I really didn't stop to think. Had I, then I'd probably have got the shakes and been completely useless. Oh, I'm a tenderfoot, all right."

Emptying his cup, Doc leaned back contentedly, tobacco smoke wreathing his cheeks.

"As a rule," he observed slowly, "I stay strictly apart from the pulling and hauling over range and grass that goes on in the territory I cover. I've seen a lot of that sort of thing and found that there's generally something to be said for both sides. However, every now and then there crops up a deal so callous and cold-blooded, I can't stomach it. You, I understand, are up against something of the sort right now with this fellow Milo Hernaman?"

Sherry nodded. "He first offered to buy me out for a small part of what the ranch is worth. When I refused to sell he made some pretty drastic threats. Today it looks as if he may have started to make some of them good. I know he has long wanted to get his hands on this ranch, but while my Uncle Jack was alive, Hernaman didn't dare start anything. Now, because as you say, I'm a tenderfoot and a woman besides, he probably feels I won't stand up to him."

"But you intend to try?"

Sherry nodded again. "There must be some kind of legal recourse to stop Hernaman, and I'm going to look for it in town tomorrow."

Doc Aden took his pipe from his mouth, surveyed the bowl thoughtfully, then tamped down the ash with a careful forefinger. "You won't find any in town, I'm afraid. I'm not at all sure you'll find it anywhere, politics and money power being what they are in the lives of men. Besides, there is a long-established point of view to contend with hereabouts. It rises from an old saying to the effect that every man should 'stomp his own snakes.' There are, of course, some things nobody will stand still for, but in the everyday give and take of range competition, the meat of that old saying guides most of our people."

"In other words," said Sherry, "what you're hinting at is that if I—or we—here at Clear Creek hope to stand up to Milo Hernaman, we must fight him alone?"

"That is what it amounts to," affirmed Doc Aden. "Fight him alone and with his own ruthless methods and weapons. Not a pleasant prospect, I admit—particularly with your being what you are."

"What am I, Doctor?"

"Why," said Doc Aden steadily, "you are a gently reared, gracious, very attractive young woman who naturally is revolted at the thought of what open conflict with Milo Hernaman might lead to in the way of further bloodshed. But I would warn you that any concern on the part of Hernaman over such a possibility simply doesn't exist. The man has a strong strain of pure brute in him that leaves no room for kinder sentiments. That is a fact you must accept and steel yourself to meet. Unless you do, I see little future for Clear Creek."

As was usual when she was worried or deeply troubled, Sherry moved about restlessly. "You put it plainly, Doctor."

Doc Aden shrugged. "There is no point in putting it otherwise. I'm sorry if I've upset you, but as one old enough to be your father, the advice I offer is well meant and, I truly believe, sound. What are Luke Casement's feelings in the matter?"

"About like yours, I'm afraid," Sherry admitted slowly. "Though he is willing that I try other means—if I can find any."

"Whatever you do," warned Doc Aden, "don't tie his hands too long. If you do, then find yourself drawn into an all out fight anyhow, it could be too late. Milo Hernaman has a favorite method of taking over range besides disposing of the rightful owner beforehand as was the case with Joe Moss. He floods that range with cattle. Unless he is stopped in time, he drowns you with cattle!"

Doc stood up and ran a match across the bowl of his pipe, his cheeks caving inward as he puffed. "Thanks for a most satisfying meal, Miss Gault. Now I'll have another look at our boy Lee before locating a handy bunk and turning in for the night."

Left to herself, Sherry went into the office and considered Doc Aden's words in somber thought. She knew she could not reasonably discount them, for they represented an objective viewpoint arrived at by intelligent observation and without personal bias. You fought Milo Hernaman with the same tools and ruthlessness he employed if you hoped to stand against him. That was how Doc Aden had put it. And, she mused bitterly, it was a responsibility and a decision that could be neither side-stepped nor shifted to other shoulders. So—what to do?

She was still brooding over the problem when Kate Larkin came in, looking tired but serene. "Lee's asleep," she reported. "Doc Aden is so confident he shooed me out, told me to go home and quit worrying. So I'll run along now, or brother Roy will think I've fallen off the edge of the world. If it's all right with you, I'll be back tomorrow."

Sherry smiled gently. "Of course. He's your man, isn't he?"

Kate's nod was vehement. "And when I think how close I came to losing him . . . !" Her eyes misted, and she blinked rapidly.

"Yes," said Sherry. "How very close! And why? Because he was looking after my interests. I think you might find cause to hate me for that."

"Hate you!" Kate exclaimed. "For heaven's sake, why? I told you before that ranch life has it's hazards, legitimate and otherwise. And while you might hate and fear them, there is no way you can completely avoid them. Our men know this, even better than we do. But if they cheerfully accept their risks, we woman can do no less. If they are strong in their way, we womenfolk must be strong in ours. And if we have to weep for them, why then we weep. We do what we have to do."

For some time after Kate left, Sherry sat quietly, reviewing again the events of the day. There had been many of them—for that matter, not only had this day been eventful, but from the moment she had first stepped off the *Overland Limited* at Battle Mountain, she had been caught up in a whirl of problems and happenings hard to reconcile and stay in balance about. It was, she thought, as though she were being rushed by some sort of wild destiny toward a decision on which her entire future could depend.

Restlessness gripped her anew. She got up and prowled the room again before opening the outer door and stepping into the night. A great stillness held the world. Lights burned in the bunkhouse and cook shack, but no sound came from them. Sheer and black against the stars loomed the rim, and the valley was filled with an inky darkness that would resolve into a sea of the purest silver once the moon rose.

The stars, it seemed, were a little higher and colder than when she had last viewed them. Well, why not? The passing of a day or two—a night or two—meant summer was that much older, winter that much nearer. Time and the world held to an immutable pace. The world had its seasons, which never paused or waited, whatever the problems of puny humans. And time swallowed up all puny humans and their problems.

Sherry hugged herself and went back into the house.

How had Kate Larkin put it? You did what you had to do. . . .

They were away for town before sunup. Doc Aden had left only minutes before Luke Casement rolled the ranch buckboard over to where Sherry stood waiting.

"Lee?" she asked.

"Weak, sore, and cranky," Casement said, grinning. "I imagine he'll manage to sweeten up a little when Kate shows later. She promised Doc Aden she'd be over, and she knows how to handle Doc's instructions. Lee figures to mend faster than Doc first thought. Doc says that love can do wonders at healing."

Sherry laughed as she settled herself on the buckboard seat, only too aware that these casual words had put color in her cheeks. This made her impatient with herself, for there was no good rea-

163

son why this should happen, or for that matter why a sort of breathless awareness should grip her whenever she was near this man.

The team had the usual amount of morning run in them, which lasted until they were well across the valley and climbing the far slope toward the turnoff leading to the Larkin headquarters. Here Kate met them, sitting her saddle with sure, casual ease.

Casement hauled up. "Your man," he reported, reading the question in her eyes, "isn't fit to live with. If you don't hurry up and get over there and sweeten him up some, the boys are liable to chuck him out of the bunkhouse on his neck, he's grown that mean."

Understanding very well that behind Casement's joshing manner and words lay the message that Lee was in good shape, Kate smiled fondly. "You're always a comfort, Mr. Casement. I've so often wondered how it was I fell in love with Lee Toland instead of you."

Casement chuckled. "Some *hombres*, like Lee, have all the luck."

When a team trotted steadily and buckboard wheels turned just as steadily, miles inevitably drifted behind. Sherry found, somewhat to her surprise and satisfaction, that the road and the country around about were becoming increasingly familiar, now that she had been this way a few times. She thought about how this could be.

A country, it seemed, had a way of absorbing you until you adjusted to it unconsciously.

The first time over the road, coming out of town to the ranch, her city-trained eyes had registered only the obvious, and she would have missed a lot of things of interest if Luke Casement had not been there to point them out to her. Now, on her own account, she was picking up the things behind the obvious—like the small, quick movements in the sage telling of the wildlife there. And once she glimpsed the white alarm hairs on the rump of a startled antelope in the middle distance before Casement did.

When she exclaimed over this, he showed her a brief smile. "You're learning," he said, and again she flushed under this brief touch of praise.

Holding to an interval of a few miles ahead, Doc Aden's livery rig funneled up a thin, amber dust cloud. Eyeing it, Sherry presently spoke her thoughts. "I think men like Doctor Aden are among the world's finest. They give much of themselves for the benefit of others. Think what it must mean to some harried husband or wife or parent, out on some far lonely ranch and in frantic need of a doctor's aid, to see him come driving in to take their burden on his capable shoulders. To them at such times he must seem almost Godlike."

"That's putting it pretty well," Casement agreed. Small grin wrinkles narrowed his eye corners. "I bet you could find a whole passel of kids

165

born within fifty miles of town who are packing the name of George. Yeah, Doctor George Aden is one of our favorite citizens."

The closer they came to town, the more impatient Sherry became to get there. So when Casement finally reined the team into the shadowy gloom of the runway of Jimmy Ink's livery barn, she was quickly out of the rig. "Where would I most likely find that sheriff you think so little of—that Broady Ives?"

Casement considered a moment. "Off hand, I'd have to say either at his office, filling his favorite chair, or propped against the bar in the Enterprise. As it happens, I crave a little talk with friend Broady myself. So I'll tag along."

Coming forward out of the stable shadows, Jimmy Ink touched a battered old Stetson to Sherry, then glanced meaningfully at Casement. He tipped his head toward the Winchester slung behind the buckboard seat and spoke laconically. "Now that's good medicine for varmints, Luke—when you got 'em out in the sage. But when they're roamin' town, a six-shooter is handier and quicker."

Alertness sharpened Casement's glance. "Now you're right there, Jimmy. But today I kind of figured they'd be out in the brush."

Sherry had moved out to the entrance of the runway, anxious to get on with the ideas that had brought her to town. Casement lowered his voice.

"Some hanging around, Jimmy?"

166

"A couple. Last I saw they headed into the Enterprise. And the boss buzzard went into Francis Quinnault's office mebbe twenty minutes ago. Luke, what's Yance Hawn doin' hangin' around with Pete Hugo? Thought Hawn was a Clear Creek hand."

"I fired him the other night, Jimmy."

"Well now," approved Jimmy Ink, "that's good riddance. And now he's gone over to Hernaman, is that it?"

"Seems so. Would you happen to have one of those short guns that a man could borrow?"

"Just so!" Jimmy ducked into his harness room and brought back a big blue .45 Colt. "Loaded and ready to go, Luke. And in top shape. I keep all of my gear that way."

Casement hefted the weapon, then tucked the gun in the waistband of his jeans, well around on the left side and out of sight under his old canvas coat. "Obliged, Jimmy," he said soberly.

"Any time, Luke," Jimmy returned. "Damn Milo Hernaman and all like him. Joe Moss was a good friend of mine. Don't let 'em get you on the hip, boy."

Casement went along and joined Sherry. She looked at him narrowly. "What was all the talk about?" she asked.

Casement shrugged. "Jimmy Ink wanted to know what Yance Hawn was doing, running around with one of Hernaman's outfit. I told him how it happened. Now let's go find Broady Ives."

167

Town activity was about average. Some half dozen saddle mounts dozed hipshot at the tie racks along the street. A big double-hitch freight outfit was pulled up in front of the Horton and Giles store, loading for some long back-country haul. A spring wagon stood just beyond it, and a buckboard and team were in front of Francis Quinnault's office.

On the porch of the Humboldt House, Mary Tyee wielded an industrious broom while trying to ignore the comments of a couple of town loafers who occupied two of the round-backed chairs lined against the hotel front. Mrs. Megarry appeared abruptly in the hotel doorway and turned a caustic tongue on the loafers, who left the porch and slouched away.

Torry Rakestraw's old redbone hound dog, asleep in the sun outside the door of Torry's saddle shop, roused as Sherry and Casement approached, and thumped a bony tail on the board sidewalk.

"It all seems quite peaceful and safe," Sherry observed. "It's hard to believe such things could take place as did the first night I was here. Sometimes it seems as though I must have dreamed it, though of course I know perfectly well that I did not. It's just hard to reconcile this kind of atmosphere with that kind of violence."

"It isn't always the noisy dog that's dangerous." Casement's glance roved the street, missing nothing of importance along it. A pair of saddle mounts in front of the Enterprise held his attention longest, these and the buckboard in front of Francis Quinnault's office. "Uh-oh!" he exlaimed. "There's our man Broady now, having his look at the town."

Standing in the doorway of his office, Sheriff Broady Ives was a thick, burly figure, his thumbs hooked in a belt drawn tight under the round of a bulging belly. He was a short-necked man with a round head set close against his shoulders. The perpetual flush on his face was due more to whiskey than exposure to sunlight. His features were heavy and settled, and there lurked in his eyes the defensive, shifty weariness of one who sat on a pinnacle of authority he neither deserved nor was capable of fulfilling.

Open to the criticism and disrespect of better men, he was ever ready to try and justify himself with bluster. He was, in fact, one of the political misfits voters occasionally inflict upon themselves because of some momentary intellectual hiatus or misplaced zeal or sentiment.

Glimpsing the approach of Casement and Sherry, he wheeled back into the protection of his office and was sitting behind the barrier of his desk when they entered. Broady Ives was a man of two faces. When he thought he could get away with it, he blustered; when he knew he couldn't, he fawned. He fawned now.

"Morning, folks—morning. Great morning,

169

ain't it? Must have been mighty fine riding in from the ranch on a morning like this. Now there was something you wanted to see me about?"

"Yes, there is," said Sherry crisply. "I want to report two cases of flagrant law violation, and I want something done about it."

Effusiveness began drying up. Broady got out a cigar and made big business of getting it ready and lighting up. His little lead-colored eyes took on their usual guarded, defensive shine.

"Well, now—ma'am, any time the law is real violated, we certainly aim to do something about it. Of course, maybe what some would call a violation, wouldn't exactly shape up that way in the eyes of the law. Now me—I always aim to get both sides of any argument before I start laying out any authority. That way—"

"Sure—sure," cut in Casement sardonically. "Everybody knows how noble you are in running your office. But suppose you shut up all the mealy-mouthed palaver and listen to what Miss Gault has to say!"

Vastly affronted, Broady tried to bristle, but he couldn't make a go of it under the scathing pressure of Casement's glance. "All right, ma'am," he mumbled sulkily. "Just what's bothering you?"

Sherry told him. She sketched the attempt at rustling she and Casement had discovered, and she told of the shooting affair at Bondurant Crossing. "Both of these things are open violations of

170

the law," she announced vigorously. "So I expect you to arrest those responsible and bring them in to face proper prosecution."

Broady's evasiveness deepened. "You understand, ma'am—that before I can go out slapping arrests on folks, I got to have proof of—"

Casement cut in again. "You got proof—plenty of it. Miss Gault's word. And mine. We both saw what we saw, heard what we heard. You locate Shag Buckholt, and you've got another witness on the rustling deal. And if you'd get up enough energy to ride out to the old Bondurant Crossing on our Clear Creek range, you'll find the carcasses of the two horses Hawn and Pete Hugo shot down. Finally, if you'll get hold of Doc Aden he'll tell you he spent the night with us at Clear Creek after taking care of the wound Yance Hawn's slug put in Lee Toland. Is that enough proof for you?"

"Still just your story," stated Broady sullenly. "How do I know Yance Hawn wasn't telling the truth when he said Jack McCord left him a little herd of cows? Maybe McCord did just that. I'd have to look over the will before I'd know different for sure. You say Hawn and Pete Hugo were caught drivin' Dollar stock onto Clear Creek range, and that without cause Yance and Pete opened up on the Toland boys. That don't make sense either. Maybe it was the other way around —the Tolands started shooting first. So!" Broady sat back, something not far from a smirk on his face, as though he felt he had come up with a perfect defense of his position and a good reason for not taking the action Sherry had requested.

Sherry faced him in angry astonishment and disbelief. "You mean," she demanded, "that in the face of the exact facts as we've given them, you intend doing nothing?"

Broady Ives shrugged. "It's like I say, ma'am. Before I can act, I got to have proof. And there ain't no real proof of anything wrong here. Just your word against the word of the other fellow. Which, as the law sees it, ain't no proof at all."

Sherry turned to Casement. "Luke, can he actually mean that?"

Casement nodded, his open contempt searing Ives. "He means it all right. It is how I expected it would be. We might as well accept the fact that friend Broady belongs to Milo Hernaman, head, hide, and horns."

"So," said Sherry, quietly intent. "Both you and Doctor Aden are right, after all. If we fight Milo Hernaman, we fight him alone. And though I want to be strong about it . . . I'm afraid, Luke—I'm afraid!"

"Don't you be," Casement told her. "So far we've been giving others first bite. Now we're all through doing that. Now it's our move. Now we get tough!"

With the words he leaned, reached a quick hand across the desk, and ripped the star from Broady Ives's shirt. When Broady, startled, would have reared up in protest, Casement drove a hard open palm against his chest, slamming him back into his chair.

"Stay put!" ordered Casement harshly. "Stay put, Broady—and listen to gospel. First, I'm throwing this star out in the street, as that's where it belongs after being pinned on you; I'd rather see it on the collar of Torry Rakestraw's old Buster dog than on you—it would mean more. Next, there's a ruckus shaping up between Clear Creek and Milo Hernaman. Seeing you've let Hernaman get away with murder—literally, for that's what it was with Joe Moss—then you damn well better not get in our way. Pin that in your hat, Broady. *Don't . . . get . . . in . . . our . . . way!* You do, you'll be treated like any other damn crook."

Broady Ives listened dazedly and just as dazedly stared at the star clenched in Casement's hand. "You can't do that," he mumbled. "You can't take my star and throw it in the street. You can't—!"

"I can't?" Casement rapped. "Watch this!" He sailed the star through the open door of the office. It struck, bounced, rolled, and tipped to a stop, half-buried. "There it is, Broady. Out in the dust. And even if you do pick it up and pin it on again, it won't mean anything. Even if you polish it for a week, it won't ever be clean again. You're all through, Broady—all through!"

Startled by Casement's abrupt actions and scalding words, Sherry awaited violent reaction

173

from Broady Ives. None came. Broady remained in his chair, beefy shoulders hunched, head lowered, a shamed and fearful man. Stripped of his star he had lost all sense of authority. Vitality had drained out of him. Without the sustaining strength of his badge of office he was suddenly a very, very little man, shrinking from reality and with no bluster or courage of any kind left in him.

Even Casement had expected something better than this from Broady. Even he had anticipated something more than a completely empty shell. He turned away, taking Sherry by the arm and steering her toward the door. "Let's get out of here. We know exactly where we stand now, and it's time to do something about it. You run along to the Humboldt House and visit with Mrs. Megarry. I've a couple of items of business to take care of."

Over the space of a scant week, Sherry had seen this man beside her in several moods. She had seen him cheerful and carefree; she had seen him thoughtful and intent; she had even seen him in bleak, explosive, destroying anger. But she had never seen him as he was now. He stood right next to her; yet he was a long way off, out on some lonely peak of dedication and icy intent. It scared her, and she caught at him.

"Luke, what are you going to do?"

"Why," he said, "I'm going to settle things— my way!"

Fear deepened in Sherry, fear not of him, but

for him. "Luke—no! There's something—something terrible in your mind. I can see it in your eyes. Luke—no! I won't have you taking on such risks! Oh, I saw what happened in the stable. That man gave you a gun, didn't he? Luke—I tell you I won't have it!"

"Be still!" He silenced her with a harshness that stunned her. "We made a compact, didn't we? That you could try your way before I tried mine? Well, you've tried yours, and you see it won't work. Now it's my turn, and you do as I say—get along to the Humboldt House!"

Abruptly he changed, even smiled. He faced her around and gave her a little push. "This is one day, gentle lady, when I give the orders."

She went along then—there was nothing else she could do. But she went with cold terror in her heart and the sting of tears in her eyes.

Chapter NINE

LUKE CASEMENT stood where Sherry Gault left him, watching until she gained the porch of the Humboldt House. Waiting, he brought out tobacco and papers and built a cigarette. He lit this and again measured the street and the significance of what it held. In particular he mused on the two saddle broncs tied in front of the Enterprise and the buckboard that stood before Francis Quinnault's office. He'd seen that buckboard on another day, with Milo Hernaman in it. Moving that way he took a final drag at his cigarette and spun the butt into the street's dust.

As he reached the office door, Francis Quinnault appeared in it, apparently about to cross the street to the Enterprise. Casement halted him with curt command. "Hold it! Let's not stir up Hawn and Pete Hugo just yet. They'll be taken care of later. Back inside, Quinnault!"

When the lawyer hesitated, as though prepared to argue, Casement cut him short. "I just reduced Broady Ives to a blob of jelly. Don't get me started on you. Inside!"

Quinnault obeyed, and Casement followed.

Milo Hernaman held down a chair beside Quinnault's desk. His big white Stetson was tipped back in the usual way, and from under it his pale eyes peered at Casement through a cloud of cigar smoke.

"Figured I'd find you here, Hernaman," Casement said. "Some things I want to talk about."

"Not interested," Hernaman grunted. "Nothing you might say now interests me."

"I wouldn't be too sure of that," Casement drawled in a soft, easy way that carried far more threat than a shout would have. "Let me jog your memory on something I told you when you came swaggering out to Clear Creek the other day with fire in your nose and your mouth full of threat and bully-puss for a young woman you're not fit to be in the same county with. I warned you then that if you—or any of your men—made any kind of strike against Clear Creek and its people, I'd waste no time on your hired bully boys. No, I wouldn't bother with them—not at first, anyway. Instead, I'd come direct to you to settle the bill."

"I don't know what you're talking about," Hernaman said, though his eyes narrowed just a little.

"Oh yes you do," retorted Casement. "You know damn well what I'm talking about. And I'm here, as I warned."

There was an enormous arrogance and self-assurance in Milo Hernaman, product of money, power, and years of an accumulating success. He had seen too many men shrink and knuckle under before him, had trampled over too many others on his way to the top, and these things had made him contemptuous toward his fellowman. Few had ever stood up to him successfully. Jack McCord had been one of them, and in consequence his memory was cordially hated by Hernaman. Now the man who had been Jack McCord's right hand faced him—Luke Casement, also cordially hated.

A strong factor in Milo Hernaman's past success had been his ability to read and correctly appraise other men, to judge the true measure of their purpose no matter what front they put on. Now, in Luke Casement, he saw something that put a knot in his belly and a stir of trepidation up his spine. He thought, studying Casement with an extreme care, that he had never before faced such a look of cold intent as was in Casement's eyes.

"Out at headquarters last night," went on Casement, "Sam Kell said something that made sense —a lot of sense. He said, Hernaman, that you'd lived too long, hurt too many people. I've been thinking about that. Sam's right. You have lived too long, and it's time something was done about it. I know you have a gun on you—a shoulder gun. You better go for it while you're able!"

He said it almost quietly, but the words wrung a breathy gasp from Francis Quinnault, who moved quickly to the far side of the room. Milo Hernaman came slowly erect, spreading his feet, squaring himself as though by the mere appearance of truculence he might carry this thing off. But in him burned the dismal conviction that here at last neither pose nor words would be enough. Yet he tried, burned by this sudden fear.

"No sense to that sort of thing, Casement. Not between you and me—no sense at all." He tried to keep his manner brusk, his tone confident. But the words ran thin and dry, as if caught in his throat. He made another attempt, frantically now. "We can square this thing. Between us we can square it. We can—"

"No," differed Casement flatly. "No we can't. Like I told Cass Dutcher before I ran him off the earth, this is for Joe Moss. For Joe Moss and Lee Toland and all the others your damn conscience-less greed killed or hurt along the trail. And the real color of your spine is beginning to show, isn't it, Hernaman? You're ready to creep and crawl. But this is one bind you don't squeeze clear of—not ever. God damn you—draw that gun!"

With the despairing certainty that there was no other out—that here was the last great gamble—Hernaman did go for a gun, ripping a hand under his coat for the weapon strapped there in a shoulder holster. He jerked the gun clear.

But now there was a gun in Casement's hand, which leveled and bellowed its great report. The impact of the big slug drove Milo Hernaman back and down, while pure reflex on his part sent a shot slashing through the ceiling of the room. A heavy mass on the floor, he made one final move, a small lift of a hand, before dropping back in limpness. Then he was very still.

Over at the Enterprise a shout lifted. Drawn by the sound, Casement moved into the open in time to see Yance Hawn and Pete Hugo coming across the street at a run. They stopped at sight of him and for a space were still, hung with indecision. Then Pete Hugo broke, pulling a gun and throwing a shot that chugged solidly into the wall beside Casement.

Pete Hugo was a squat, swarthy shape out there in the hard glare of the sun. Knowing he had missed with his first shot, he tried another hurriedly—too hurriedly, for he missed with it too. Before he could attempt a third, Casement fired, sighting deliberately. A leg went out from under the Dollar foreman, letting him down in a tangled sprawl, where he lay cursing and scrabbling about, with all the fight knocked out of him.

Caught up completely now with the black madness of this thing, Casement moved to turn his gun on Yance Hawn, but at that moment Hawn's first try seared like white fire across the heavy muscles of Casement's forearm, shocking his gun from his grasp.

In a sort of numbed calm he looked at the arm and the quick rush of blood flooding his wrist and hand. Then he leaned and tried to pick the gun up again, but there was no power in his fingers, and the weapon slipped from his blood-slimed grip. He reached for the gun with his left hand as Hawn's second slug drove a burst of splinters from the hitch rail, setting the buckboard team rearing and fighting their tie ropes.

Hawn came ahead three quick steps, lifting his gun for a sure third try. But from down street at Jimmy Ink's livery barn a rifle snarled its hard, flat challenge and a bullet ripped the dust at Hawn's feet, before howling away in banshee ricochet. Shaken by this unexpected menace, Hawn missed his try, then turned and raced for the saddle mounts at the Enterprise hitch rail. Up on one of them, he spurred away, crouched low in the saddle.

Again the flat challenge of the rifle set the echoes winging, and an invisible force lifted Yance Hawn and drove him far out along the neck of his speeding mount. For a jump or two he stayed so, then rolled off, slamming into the street's dust, limp and broken.

A rush of movement brought Casement around, and then Sherry Gault was clinging to him, whimpering like a hurt child, her words part broken sobs, part choked incoherencies, with only his name clearly uttered, over and over again.

"Oh, Luke, Luke, Luke . . . !"

Small, wiry, and waspy, and still carrying Casement's Winchester, Jimmy Ink came charging up. Then came others, drawn by the sound of gunfire. Dan Vincent, spare and straight and grizzled, left his bank, and Curt Giles came from his store. And Doc Aden, who had answered the summons of this sort of thing many times before, came and took over with crisp professional authority.

In his office he made swift repairs on Casement's arm before going to work on Pete Hugo, who had been carried into a back room. Still shaken, but quieted now, Sherry stood beside Casement as Doc worked, and as he finished, Doc gave her arm a squeeze.

"Remember what I told you, my dear. In this country men stomp their own snakes and do what they have to do. So no regrets, please. Just be thankful for your luck—and Luke's. Now get him over to the hotel, where he can take it easy for a while. I'll be around for another look at him before I send him home."

The reaction had hold of Casement now, and he was held in a gray depression. It wasn't only the effect of his wound; it was even more the aftermath of the dark fury that had scourged him during the wicked moments just passed. That kind of anger was a fire that could make an emotional cinder out of a man, draining him of all capacity for feeling of any kind.

Mrs. Megarry, wise in the way of a man's needs at such times, sat Casement in a quiet corner of her own private parlor and brought him three fingers of rye whiskey.

To Sherry she said, " 'Tis an exhaustion that needs time for passing. And best to let him find his own way back."

Sherry pulled a chair up beside him and sat quietly, until presently Casement spoke, his words low.

"Just so you don't hate me for it. I could see it as the only thing—the only way out. The man would accept no other answer. Just so you don't hate me . . . !"

"No, Luke," she told him, hardly above a whisper, for the thickness of her past fears was still in her throat. "Not that, Luke—not ever."

"Makes you wonder," he went on slowly. "Makes you wonder what it is in a man's makeup to set him off like that. Some sort of pressure that finally breaks loose—turns him wild and savage."

He shook his head wearily. "Leaves a big bill to pay."

After a bit, Jimmy Ink sidled in, and Casement showed him a small, grim smile. "I had to buy in, Luke," said the little livery owner. "I knew they were set to two-time you, so when I saw Hawn and Pete Hugo come across the street rollin' smoke, I knew it was you they were cutting down on. So I grabbed your Winchester off the buckboard and bought in. I don't recollect thinkin' too clear about it—about what I did and why I did. I just—just did, that's all."

"And because you did is why I'm sitting here right now, Jimmy. For the rest of my life I'll be thanking you."

"You don't owe me no thanks," said Jimmy stoutly. "You're my good friend, ain't you?"

When Jimmy Ink left, Sherry spoke, her voice steadier and clearer. "You are his good friend— so he did what he did. To him that was all he wanted—or was needed. Just that you were his good friend. I keep getting lessons in values, Luke."

The next to show were Dan Vincent and Curt Giles. These were the town's two big men, the banker and the merchant. Their opinions would be the town's opinions, their voices the voices of the town. So now Casement put his glance on them, and in it was a searching question that Dan Vincent recognized and answered.

"One of those things, Luke. Men like Milo

Hernaman always meet up with the same answer, some in one way, some in another. They never seem to understand that you can push other people only so far. So take good care of that arm. I see some good seasons ahead."

Later on, it was Doc Aden again, to make sure his first hurried care of Casement's arm had been good. As he worked he reported on Pete Hugo. "He's due to end up with a leg that will be a reminder for the rest of his life that today he was a damn fool. He admitted they were laying for you, Luke." He fashioned a sling for the wounded arm. "I'll be out at the ranch in a couple of days for another look at Lee Toland. I'll check up on this arm again then. As it is now, I see no good reason why you shouldn't take it home with you."

They left in the early afternoon. At the livery barn, Casement took the near side of the buckboard seat. "You're driving," he told Sherry. "Chance for you to practice handling a team."

She found it wasn't too difficult. For the most part, once clear of town the team pretty well drove themselves, setting their own pace, trotting for a time, walking a little, then trotting again. The sun came down strongly, but it was a good heat, a comforting heat, easing away tensions and luring the mind into a peaceful repose.

They had ridden a considerable distance in silence before Sherry spoke. "I wouldn't have believed it, that after that first awful impact it now

184

begins to blur a little, to fade. Does it mean that I've become completely callous, Luke?"

"Not at all," he assured her. "You're getting a proper perspective, that's all. Sure, it's the sort of thing no normal person willingly mixes in, but it's one of those things life throws at you, and you have to face it. Now it is part of the back trail—another rough spot to climb over. With distance, any picture begins to fade. And there is in it the healing power of time. If these things were not so, they'd be no lift, no joy in life at all."

She looked at him. He was slouched down, finding a loose ease. The hardness and bitterness had left his face.

"Again the cowboy philosopher is with us," she said lightly.

He grinned. "Being with you brings out such thoughts in a man."

She flushed and took cover. "I must think about that."

When they topped the west crest of Clear Creek valley, Sherry pulled the team to a halt. "I want to look at it again, Luke—and see if it means now what it did the first time I saw it."

It was all there, just as it had been before. Just as it would always be. And it now meant not just as much as before, but more. For now there was no shadow of threat over it.

As they dropped down into the valley, Sherry spoke slowly. "I've the strongest feeling of—of coming home, Luke. Back East it was never quite this way. Oh, I had a home there and it sheltered me in comfort, but somehow it was different. Somehow it didn't seem to mean what it does here. There you were never out of sight of others, and in your daily activity you simply moved from one building to another. But here—well, the word 'home' means more." She considered for a moment, then shook her head. "That may sound silly —but there is a difference."

"Sure there is," Casement agreed. "Here you may never see a house in a day of work until you head back to your own. Then, when you catch first sight of it, it's really home—a haven in all the great emptiness around you. Oh, I know what you mean, all right."

They went on across the flats, across the creek ford, and up the far slope to headquarters. The McCabe shepherd came barking, and this alarm brought Kate Larkin to the bunkhouse door, where she swiftly got the significance of Sherry's doing the driving. She dropped a remark across her shoulder, and when she came forward Griff Toland followed her out.

As Sherry reined to a halt, Kate's direct scrutiny was on the sling supporting Casement's arm. "And just what kind of mischief have you been up to, Mr. Casement?" Her tone was light, but the concern behind it wasn't.

"A little argument over the rights of men,"

186

Casement divulged carefully. "How's our boy Lee?"

"Bossy," said Kate tersely. "Wants to feed himself and sulks because I won't let him. Now just what was this about the rights of men?"

Casement evaded direct answer by looking past her at Griff Toland. "Where are Sam Kell and Al Birch, Griff?"

"Ridin' our south line. Hopin' to meet up with some of Hernaman and company—especially Yance Hawn and Pete Hugo."

"They won't," Casement told him succinctly. "After you put up the team you can go call them in."

As Griff led the team away, Casement turned to Sherry. "I'd say you'd made the grade, gentle lady—all the way." He was half-smiling, but there was a drawn gauntness about his cheeks.

"I wouldn't know about that," Sherry returned. "But this I am sure of—you, sir, are not made of iron. So here is an order—go get some rest."

He weighed the idea for a slow, sober moment. Then he nodded. "Think I will—a little."

He went into the bunkhouse, and Kate, watching him, came around to Sherry anxiously. "Whatever happened, he's trying to make it of small account, but he's not fooling me. I know that man. His arm isn't all that is hurt. Deep inside he's all bruised and scarred. Now suppose you tell me the truth. What happened?"

Sherry told it as best she could, and this reviving of the dark and savage moments of a supreme accounting thickened her throat again. "And—and afterward," she ended almost tearfully, "he said to me, 'Just so you don't hate me for it.'" She could hardly get the words out. "As if I could —as if I ever could!"

Kate put an arm around her. "Of course—as though you ever could." Still for a thoughtful moment, Kate went on. "I suppose I should be surprised, but somehow I'm not. Because it is so like him—the will to do what he felt had to be done. Yes, so like him. The quiet, tolerant man—the basically kind man. There are some like that, a brave few who can be so terrible in their wrath when finally fully aroused against injustice. And Luke Casement has always been one of such."

Quiet then for a time while considering the full significance of what she'd heard, Kate looked around with quickening spirit. "How bright the sun; how clear the day!" she exclaimed.

Filled with its shaded quiet, the ranch house was a sanctuary that Sherry Gault clung to for the rest of the day.

Earlier than she had yesterday, Kate Larkin rode off homeward, still caught up with the momentous news she was carrying.

Sherry had the most frugal of suppers, then watched evening settle in with its blue, gentle dusk while the first stars began to glint and flicker.

188

Later, in the full darkness, she threw a wrap about her shoulders and went out to stand under those stars and make silent obeisance to the great black majesty of the rim.

She walked as far as the corrals, and there he came up beside her, just as he had that first night when she stepped off the *Overland Limited*.

"Thought you might be out," he said. "Some things need settling between you and me. You mind?"

Why the quick warmth in her cheeks—why the breathless awareness? Would it always be this way?

"No," she said, her voice very small and not quite steady. "No, Luke. I don't mind. These things—what are they?"

"Like this," he said. "After the shoot-out, when you came to me, there were things in your voice more than just words. In the touch of your hands, too—saying things words couldn't. All this I thought was real. Was I mistaken?"

She was very still—still until his sound arm was around her and she was drawn close.

"Was I, gentle lady—was I mistaken?"

She reached up and pulled his head down to her. "No, Luke—you were not mistaken. And if I hadn't found you there—still straight, still strong —I think I would have died too. . . ."

189

L. P. Holmes was the author of a number of outstanding Western novels. Born in a snowed-in log cabin in the heart of the Rockies near Breckenridge, Colorado in 1895, Holmes moved with his family when very young to northern California and it was here that his father and older brothers built the ranch house where Holmes grew up and where, in later life, he would live again. He published his first story—*The Passing of the Ghost*—in *Action Stories* (9/25). He was paid $1/2$¢ word and received a cheque for $40. 'Yeah—forty bucks' he said later. 'Don't laugh. In those far-off days . . . a pair of young parents with a three-year-old son could buy a lot of groceries on forty bucks.' He went on to contribute nearly 600 stories of varying lengths to the magazine market as well as to write over fifty Western novels under his own name and as Matt Stuart. For the many years of his life, Holmes would write in the mornings and spend his afternoons calling on a group of friends in town, among them the blind Western author Charles H. Snow whom Lew Holmes always called 'Judge' Snow (because he was Napa's Justice of the Peace 1920–1924) and who frequently makes an appearance in later novels as a local justice in Holmes's imaginary Western communities. Holmes's Golden Age as an author was from 1948 through 1960. During these years he produced such notable novels as *Desert Range, Black Sage, Summer Range, Dead Man's Saddle,* and *Somewhere They Die* for which he received the Golden Spur Award from the Western Writers of America. In these novels one finds the themes so basic to his Western fiction: the loyalty which unites one man to another, the pride one must take in his work and a job well done, the innate generosity of most of the people who live in Holmes's ambient Western communities, and the vital relationship between a man and a woman in making a better life.